I0831912

How Whiskey Made the Coyote Sing

By Joshua Erickson

A Shelterbelt Media LLC. Print

Cover art by Emma Hiyashi

1st Edition, 2025

For S,
I can't save you.
I can't save anyone.

"Surely I haven't suffered, simply that I, my crimes and my sufferings, may manure the soil of the future harmony for somebody else. I want to see with my own eyes the hind deer lie down with the lion and the victim rise up and embrace his murderer. I want to be there when every one suddenly understands what it has all been for. All the religions of the world are built on this longing, and I am a believer. But then there are the children, and what am I to do about them? That's a question I can't answer. For the hundredth time I repeat, there are numbers of questions, but I've only taken the children, because in their case what I mean is so unanswerably clear. Listen! If all must suffer to pay for the eternal harmony, what have children to do with it, tell me, please? It's beyond all comprehension why they should suffer, and why they should pay for the harmony. Why should they, too, furnish material to enrich the soil for the harmony of the future? I understand solidarity in sin among men. I understand solidarity in retribution, too; but there can be no such solidarity with children. And if it is really true that they must share responsibility for all their fathers' crimes, such a truth is not of this world and is beyond my comprehension."

–*The Brothers Karamozov*, Fyodor Dostoyevsky

Part I

"Cowboys ain't easy to love and they're harder to hold
And they'd rather give you a song than diamonds or gold"

–WAYLON JENNINGS

1

I'VE SET OUT TO SING you a death song. I've set out to tell you the truth, and the truth is that my father drank whiskey in the truck, but I loved him anyway. Most of what you'll read about me is summed up right there. He was the man he was, but I loved him. My father was the last real cowboy. He wore pearl snap shirts. He could draw from a leather holster, quick as lightning. He could lead a horse to water, though not even he could make it drink.

Now, I look back at a time long gone by, from a city that can't sleep, and there's something like nostalgia if it got sick. Back then I'd say it wasn't his fault, the life we lived. I'd say there was good about growing up the way I did. I knew more than any other girl in the world. That's another truth. I knew that brown bottles could look beautiful when the sunshine came through tinted windows and illuminated the plastic containers littering the floor of that old Chevy. I knew how to change a clutch on a 4440. I knew that the song of the prairie only sang for you if you were completely yourself. Later, I would learn what could make that song incomplete.

My father introduced himself as Paul Bauer, but I always called him Papa Paul. I'd say it fast and smooshed together. Papapaul. Papapaul drank. He played cards and sang Tom Petty songs and gave the best hugs in the whole world. And he drank. But I loved him anyway.

When I lived with him, we would spend all the time in the world together and mostly it was alright. He owned a ranch out by Lemmon, a town named after a sour fruit. It sits along a paved road, in the middle of a grass ocean. The town lives and dies by the cattle that congregate along the barbed fences. Life was different there, as much the place as the time, more slow. Ranchers rarely hurry to get with the times. Many families in town didn't even have TVs when I was that age, though I didn't learn that until I met Correy. When life gives you lemons, you make lemonade. When life puts you in Lemmon, you do what you can to get by, I guess.

That's not the truth, you know. About the name. Lemmon wasn't named after the fruit. You could probably tell because of the extra M and all. Lemmon was named for George Edward Lemmon, a rancher born in 1857 according to the town's website. But the truth as a kid is something that can be whatever you need it to be.

Lemmon is up on the border of North and South Dakota. It's a cowboy town. Papapaul ranched to the east, near the reservation border. He was a real man of the prairie, a real John Wayne, even if that ranch never made a dime. Part of that was the cattle we ran, more rib than ribeye. Mostly, though, it was the fact that my father never really cared for animals. The money, and he'd tell you as much if you ever found him belly up to a bar, was in equipment.

Paul Bauer knew equipment the way a bird knows to fly south. The way a ranch hand knows to move down the line at the sound of a rattle. The way a bullet knows to find a gut. He knew machines naturally. He knew which transmission would shell out after four thousand hours and which diesel was actually made for a truck and then just stuffed into a red tractor for the sake of glorified dick-measuring. He knew them much better than he knew how to be a father, but that didn't matter until later.

The man himself was tall, at least in my eyes. Looking back, he wasn't so big, not really. I was just little, is all. Paul Bauer stood tall in my eyes, and for a while, he could do no wrong. I loved him, loved his pearl-snap pink shirts, the everpresent chin whiskers that would scratch your cheek when he hugged you, the smell of tobacco that almost overpowered his cheap aftershave. He prided himself, in those early years, on his appearance. Paul spent what felt like hours in front of the mirror, perfecting the combover, brushing the dentures.

He had dentures because he was old for a father. I suppose that's perspective. Abraham in the Bible was a hundred. Paul was only sixty-two, but he had long passed the days when he should have had a daughter. But he had me and a belief that a father should care for a daughter, even when her "no-good-bitch" mother didn't send the child support.

He never said stuff like that sober. Just when he'd have too much, and he'd always say sorry after.

The house could have been a palace to young eyes. I had a whole room all to myself, and a record player he bought me one Christmas. Like all good cowboys and cowgirls, we'd listen to Marty Robbins or Waylon Jennings.

During rainstorms, when the roof would leak and the house would creak, he'd look at me with glassy eyes and say, "Go get your records, Rosie." And I would, and we'd listen to them all through the night until we both passed out on the couch. Music was our way of connecting. We jammed to the same tune, we beat our hearts in sync with the beat, we knew how to dance a two-step.

My name isn't Rosie, by the way. My name is Samantha Rose Bauer. Only Papapaul and Corey called me Rosie, except sometimes Papa called me Lemondrop. The rest of the world called me Sam or Samantha, which suited me just fine.

Samantha Rose Bauer. Samantha's my mama's name. I never met her except one day in court when I was older. My mama never did look me in the eye. She told the state to keep me. I don't know if she's still alive today. We got by without her. It didn't bother me, not if you'd asked me then. Paul taught me how to lie, too.

As a daughter, you need a father. It wouldn't occur to me until years and many miles had separated us that maybe Paul needed a daughter.

Everything in my little life didn't come unraveled all at once. The good times tie themselves in with the bad, and the bad doesn't show up so fast. It happened slowly, like disease making its way through a herd. The heads dropped a few at a time, and the worry built up a little at a time. The first metaphor cow keeled over at a sale.

***

I THINK I was five when he first took me to a sale. I was so excited I could barely stop shaking. He told me the evening before, and I don't think I slept the entire night. Before then, Papa would get me to stay with Grandma Helen, who was Corey's grandma and not mine. I don't think I ever met him those years, but who knows? Memory is funny at that age. I do remember that she gave me the creeps, even before the motorcycle accident.

That night I stared at my ceiling, the brown lines criss-crossing across the white, and I imagined them to be highways carrying eighteen-wheelers all across the prairie. I imagined them carrying me across the prairie. By morning I had such bags under my eyes that at first Papa thought I'd got sick. It took an eternity of begging just for me to get in the front seat of his truck. By the time we hit the pavement, I'd already fallen asleep.

The truck hit a bump somewhere north of Brookings, and the gooseneck rattled, and I woke up. Papa looked at me and grinned outside his mouth. It was a trick he'd do often. All the other kids found it disturbing. He'd pop out his dentures and smile with them halfway outside his lips, and even half asleep I fell into a fit of giggling.

"Hey, Lemondrop," he said, popping the teeth back in. I stretched and my knuckles hit the corner of the headliner.

"Hey, papa," I said back. My mouth felt dry. "I'm thirsty."

He nodded and pulled a plastic bottle from a cup holder. He spit his tobacco into it and held it out as if to offer it to me. I scrunched up my face.

"Gross!"

"You don't want it?" He said, a smile tugging at the corners of his mouth.

"Can I get a pop?" He pretended to think, but I knew he would say yes. Papa had a sweet tooth too.

"Ok. But only a can, not a bottle. And after you eat breakfast."

"Where are we going for breakfast?"

As if to answer me, he turned on his blinker and crossed a lane of traffic. The car there, a great boxy thing that carried a woman who should have had her license taken a decade ago, had to nearly stop. I imagined she adjusted her glasses and said a word like 'shithead' before apologizing to Jesus for saying it.

We pulled into a service station. A green dinosaur out front had recently been repainted, and even though the paint couldn't have been more than a month old, someone had carved their initials into the side. Papa drove right up to the pump, let out a disgusting belch that made me giggle, and began pumping fuel.

I got out and stretched my arms as high as they could go. The morning air was cool against my skin, and I shivered. The station, like most buildings in that part of the world, was a squat, square thing built for function rather than style. Most people who settled there in the late 1800s and early 1900s didn't have time to think about things like artistic architecture. They were too busy trying not to freeze to death.

Autumn on the prairie felt like freezing to death, like dying. The wind howls across the open field, and the gasoline splatters on the ground and fills your nostrils, and you know in your bones, even if you're five years old you know, that the cold is coming and it'll stay awhile. The people who call a land like that home never leave it, not really. It never leaves them, neither.

People think kids are too stupid to know these things, but they aren't.

Especially not poor kids.

Papa finished filling up. He returned the ugly green nozzle to its home and drove the truck in a great arc, parking in the gravel lot next to the station. Even living in New York for over a decade now, I wonder at how a place can survive without gravel. It was everywhere out there. It's nowhere here, like we try to cover up the earth itself and somehow spare ourselves the knowledge that we're all going back into it.

When he got out of the pickup, I waited for him at the corner of the building. As he walked passed, I grabbed his hand and swung it back and forth, and he laughed, a deep-throated laugh. We stepped into the restaurant.

Blue walls. The ugliest baby blue your mind can think of, with navy-colored booths and for some ungodly reason, red-topped tables. An actual, genuine head of a deer on the south wall. Three pheasants frozen forever in mid-flight. Terry Redlin prints. When we sat down, I drank the entire place in. We were hours from home, and to a five-year-old, it might have been the moon. A young girl with black lipstick came to take our order.

"Do you do food here?" Paul asked as if it were a funny joke.

The teenager only blew a bright pink bubble with her chewing gum.

"Okay. I'll do a hamburger steak, and over easy-eggs. And a stack of pancakes for her."

"Can you put sprinkles on them?" I asked. Papa always put sprinkles on my pancakes at home.

"We don't have sprinkles," the girl said. She looked at Paul. "Coffee?"

"With cream and sugar, please." She blew another bubble. "Anything else?"

"Nope." The waitress walked away. Paul muttered under his breath, "Bitch".

He saw me looking at him and rubbed his face with his hand. "Don't use that word, sweetie. Do as I say, not as I do, okay?"

"Okay," I said. I had no idea what he meant.

2

THE PANCAKES CAME OUT COLD, and I didn't really forgive the girl for not finding sprinkles, but I ate them anyway. Halfway through, Papa got up and went to the bathroom. The waitress never checked on us, but when he stood, her eyes followed him all the way to the hallway. When he had locked the door, she scurried right up to the table.

"Hi," she said. I said nothing. I was still sore about the sprinkles. She tried again. "Hi, there."

"Hello, ma'am," I said because Papa taught me to be polite. She smiled, revealing crooked, stained teeth.

"What's your name?"

"I'm Sam. Short for Samantha."

"That's a pretty name," she said without looking at me. I knew she hadn't really listened. She just waited for her turn to talk. I felt talked down to, which I knew even at that age, didn't feel so good. So I squinted up my eyes at her. "Are you...how do you know that man?"

Of all the questions I expected, that wasn't even on my radar.

"Papa?"

"Mr. Bauer."

"He's my dad," I said. She gave me a funny face, and I couldn't tell what it meant. I pointed at the book she held in her left hand. "Whatcha reading?"

"Where do you live?" She hadn't even answered my question, and it felt odd that she was so interested in my life. People around the ranch didn't ask questions like that. Of course, everyone around us knew where our ranch was, and she had never been there.

"We live in Lemmon. It's..." I realized I had no idea which direction we had come from. "It's a long way away." The toilet flushed, and the waitress moved quicker than most grown-ups did. I know because they always told me to slow down even though they moved about as fast as wandering cows themselves. By the time Papa opened the door, she sat in the corner with her book open, as if she had never moved. The only difference was her hands: they shook.

Some part of the odd waitress spooked me. The way she didn't come any nearer than she had to. The way she snatched up the check too fast to be polite. I saw once, years later, a dog in a shelter who had been beaten horribly. The girl, if you'll forgive such a cruel simile, looked a lot like that dog.

We finished our meal and got back in the truck. My brain ran off on me, an unbroken mustang let out of the corral. I forgot all about the pop, and the sprinkles, and even the waitress. Like so many things when you're that age, the girl who took our order became just another unexplained part of life. My little mind had too much to occupy it, and though I haven't thought about her for quite some time, I do remember that seeing her with that paperback stirred something in my stomach. Papa whistled a tune down the highway, and I thought that I would very much like to learn to read.

***

IF YOU HAVEN'T been to an auction, you probably think you have an idea of what it's like. I know I had my own expectations. I had seen an auctioneer once on TV, up on a maple podium, talking like he had just gotten a tongue and wanted to make up for fifty years of lost time. Numbers upon numbers upon numbers. Most kids learned to count with toys or flashcards. I learned in hundred-dollar increments chanted over a cattle crowd. *Four hundred. Four hundred. Would ya bid five? Five hundred. Five gotta be six hundred. Six hundred. Six hundred. Six hundred. I'll trade with you, sir, five fifty.*

Over and over and over. That's what I saw on TV. But it wasn't the real thing.

In reality, the auctioneer had a funny handlebar mustache that reminded me of a Pringles can. It hung above his prominent upper lip, a gray hat for bright white teeth. The man's name was Lionel Richards. Everyone called him "Big Rich", a fitting name for a man of his size. Except Paul. Paul had a way of nicknaming everyone a little differenty. He called the man "Lionel Richy" after the musician at first. Sometime before my time, it got shortened to just Richy, which the auctioneer hated, but Paul bought well, so he didn't say anything.

We parked the truck next to a line of diesel pickups. In the distance, a ramshackle farmhouse that made our home look like a palace. A red barn, at least at one point it had been red, leaned to the left. Lines of weeds stood taller than my head. In front of us, all arrayed and done up in their Sunday best, sat a dozen green tractors, the nicest things in the whole place. Even the growing group of people looked worn and weathered in their flannels and their greasy hats. The tractors, though. They looked as bright as any playground to me.

"Richy," my dad shouted as we walked up to the crowd, and ignored the slight reddening of the massive man's jowls.

"Paul," he said, extending a hand that my father's practically disappeared inside of. "You look at the flier we mailed out."

"Yeah," Papa said, looking down the line of machinery. He was in his element, and to me, it looked like someone had wound him up and let him go. He glanced around, his mind a calculator assessing decades of data. "That old Alice. What do you know?"

"You might want to steer clear of that one." Rich patted his pocket. "It doesn't run. And I've got a fair amount of bids already."

"Does it have the three point?"

"Yep. 540 PTO."

"Hours?"

"Unknown."

"What about the old M?"

"Starts, needs a new battery."

"That's the next guy's problem."

"That's the auctioneer's line," Lionel said, and they both laughed. Confused, but not wanting to be left out, I laughed too. Lionel jumped. "Oh. Sorry. I didn't see you there. Is this..."

"Sam, say hello," Papa said. I took a step forward, and copying what my father had done earlier, extended a hand. Lionel took it carefully and shook it once.

"I'm Lionel. What's your name?"

"Sam. It's short for Samantha Rose," I said, and I was happy to see he actually listened. I liked Lionel from then on. It's rare that grown-ups actually listen to a kid.

The auction started on four old flatbed trailers. People picked through cardboard flats of rusty wrenches, drills with frayed chords, boxes of half-used spray paints. A few of them smoked cigarettes. The cool morning air didn't keep many of the old men in their pickups. One in a greasy jumpsuit tried to talk to me, and I got scared, and I ran back to Papa. He didn't have much interest in the small items. A saw here, a rake there, Papa called that stuff "small peanuts". He bid a box of old playboys up to twenty dollars before leaving it to one of the immense characters in a hat that should have been worn by a Confederate soldier.

Lionel kept watch over the crowd from a pickup bed camper. They had cut a window in the side and written "Richard's Auctions" in great maroon bubble letters across both sides. His chant sounded slow to me, who had only ever seen cattle auctioned. He stayed on numbers longer, playing farmer off of farmer. Sometime before they got through the last trailer of "small peanuts", Papa and I wandered to an old horse trailer converted into a restaurant-on-wheels. He bought himself a cup of coffee and a hot chocolate for me. The lady behind the counter put on a lot of marshmallows and winked in my direction.

We went back just as they sold the last of the small items, a mower with a bag on the back that was more hole than fabric, which brought $2.50.

"Folks," Lionel said in his broad voice, "We're going to switch over to the machinery side in just a moment. Go ahead and grab yourself a bite to eat from our tremendous food vendor over on the east side of the property, warm up with some coffee, and we'll keep rolling along."

That's one of the first times I knew that my dad was smarter than most people. He had beaten the line of old farmers, with their droning 'uhs...' and 'ums...' and their twenty-cent tips.

The auction kept rolling along, just like Lionel said. I tried to keep all my questions stored up inside. I didn't want to interrupt Papa. He rarely looked this way around the farm; concentrated, busy, full of life. Instead I just drank in every detail I could. The way the mud seeped into my tennis shoe when I made a wrong step. The smell of too much cologne on another machinery jockey. The glitter of a gold watch on a man wearing a tattered jumpsuit. The world felt so real there, so crafted. It didn't feel like the prairie we lived on, where God had made rattlesnakes and prairie grass and everything in between. This was creation muddied, creation filled with leaning people and machine grease. God made Adam and Eve and the holy book. We made the barn rotting, the ancient Ford in the weeds, the cigarette. Even so, it had a type of charm. It came from the fact that Paul Bauer was one of them.

I loved all the people so much. They were real, genuine people, each with something different to offer the world. I'd never known just how different a world could be, and instead of frightening, it was wonderful.

***

PAPA BOUGHT THE Allis Tractor for three thousand four hundred and fifty dollars, and I forgot thinking he was smart a few hours before. When I had been four, I thought I was rich after finding three whole quarters. A hundred dollars was unthinkable. I thought Papa had sold the farm to afford that machine.

He made me wait in the truck while a man with a thermos full of more whiskey than coffee loaded the trailer. They used a winch and a yellow skid steer to push it onto the trailer. Papa passed the man a bill in a handshake and began throwing chains around the axles of the tractor. Paul Bauer never had a clean vocabulary, but when he chained machinery down, his words were downright diabolical. He swore on the lives of saints and the risque body parts of Mother Mary and cursed my mother and used slurs for races that didn't even live near us. When it came to racism, my father was quite the world traveler. We took off down the road, and I didn't speak for five minutes just to be sure he wouldn't turn his spout of swearing on me.

I didn't need to worry. He was in a better mood now that we were driving back.

"What'd you think, Rosie? You have fun?"

"Yeah," I said, and meant it. Then, before I could stop myself, the questions came running. "Is that always where they have auctions? Why did the one man not have any underwear on? Didn't he know people could see his buttcrack when he bent over? Did Lionel mean to say 'shit' in the microphone?" And then, before he could answer any of them, "Why did we spend so much money on that orange tractor?"

Papa's eyes gleamed the way they did before he told me about how rattlers knew where to lay eggs or how John Wayne always knew where the bad guys were going. He knew something I didn't, and he wanted to share.

"That old man I bid against, he's a sucker. So is the farmer." Papa rolled down the window, and the cold air made me shiver. He lit a Camel cigarette. I was tired of the smell of tobacco, but I wanted to know the answer more than I wanted to give my nose a break. "The world has two kinds of people in it. There's good folks, and there's suckers. People call them different names wherever you go, but everybody knows that there's only those two people. Good folks know what's good for them. They know to pay attention. They mind their manners. They say please and thank you."

He took a draw and tried to blow it out the window. The wind carried most of it back through the window and over to me anyway.

"Suckers, on the other hand, they don't look out for themselves. They let other people do the work for them. They don't learn about the world." He jabbed a thumb at the tractor behind us. "I can sell that machine for ten thousand dollars. Because I know what it is, and I know there's a rancher about a hundred miles from us who's been looking for one because he grew up on it." Papa laughed to himself, and I didn't know what was funny.

"You pay attention to me, honeybee. I'll teach you all about how the world works. But if you're going to learn, you'll have to want to learn. Nobody can teach you that."

We rode along. He put in a Tom Petty cassette tape. As the first words of the song came over the radio, I decided what kind of person I wanted to be. I wanted to be someone who learned. The sound of our voices sailed out across the open fields all the way home.

3

YOU CAN'T SING THIS SONG without Corey. Corey Bruce Hoffman. He's the one who told me that you introduce people by their full names. I didn't, and don't, think that it's all that important for people to know that my middle name is Rose, or that his middle name was Bruce, but I do it anyway. Of all the people in my life, no one has had an effect like Corey did. When I first learned that B.C. meant Before Christ, I created a map of my own life in the same way. Those first seven years were "Before Corey".

I knew Corey from before, but we didn't really spend time together. I would see him around the town when he would visit during the summers, sometimes at the grocery store, sometimes at the petrified wood park, but that was all. He went to live full-time with Grandma Helen the year I turned seven, and when I asked papa why, he told me to hush up, and I did.

He had blonde hair in a perpetual state of overgrowth. His Grandmother, Grandma Hellen, had hands that shook more than grass in a tornado. There had been an accident, and now only one of those hands remained. She clipped his hair once a year, and never without leaving at least two nicks to be covered by bandages later. When I met him, the last of his baby teeth had just fallen out. His front teeth. He had the biggest gap, all gum in the grin, and his smile caused me to laugh because of it.

Corey Bruce Hoffman was my friend. My best friend in the whole world.

Even better, he went to school.

I'd asked Papa about school a year before. He said I could go, or I could keep driving on the road with him and learning that way. Even at seven, I could hold a light in a machine shop, I could change oil almost all by myself, and I could drive a manual so long as I could reach the pedals or had someone else to run them. Papa gave me an education that no one else could. But Papa couldn't read, not well anyways.

And I wanted to read so badly it hurt sometimes.

Corey walked his bike onto our property one Saturday afternoon. Papa slept on a great blue recliner. It was the beginning of summertime. Corey couldn't have lived with Grandma Helen more than a month. I wouldn't have even known it if I hadn't seen him around her restaurant the week before.

His back tire held on, but just barely, and the chain had come undone.

I sat on the deck, cutting an apple with a pocket knife. I saw him coming from a ways off. He came from the direction of the Bar J, a restaurant built into an old service station about twenty minutes from our house. Papa went there on Sundays and bought me ice cream while he and Grandma Helen went into a back room to talk business. Corey never spoke to me there, but I'd caught him staring at me a couple of times.

He got the bicycle up the hill and took a moment to catch his breath.

"Hi," he said brightly.

"Howdy," I said. I did my best cool cowboy impression, leaning back in my chair and popping a slice of apple in my mouth.

"You're Rosie," he said. I let my chair drop onto four legs.

"Only my papa calls me Rosie," I said, trying to sound tough.

"Why?"

I stopped. I'd never even thought why he was the only one to call me that.

"Because...because he's the most important person ever," I said. "To me," I added. Corey would know my dad wasn't an actor or a president.

"Oh. That makes sense. Can I call you Rosie if I'm important too?"

"I guess. But..." I don't know why, but it felt odd for a stranger to be calling me Rosie. "But you'd have to earn it."

"Well, what do I call you until then?"

"You can call me Sam."

"Sam's a boy's name."

"Samantha isn't," I snapped.

"Okay," he said, and in his mind, we were friends. That was what it was like with him. He knew your name, and then you were his friend.

Corey leaned his bike away from his body as if to say '*would you look at this shit*?' He had the air of adulthood about him, even then, a sort of resignation to the realities of life. Corey accepted the world and learned to laugh at the trivialities.

"I think I need help fixing my bike. Is your dad around?"

"Dad's sleeping," I said in a kinder tone. A little suspicion still hid behind the words. We didn't get visitors to the ranch, and I wasn't accustomed to another person suddenly in this space made for two. A part of me liked it though, the arrival of a new thing to break the recurring monotony of whiskied mornings and long snores in the afternoon.

And Corey went to school.

I'll admit, even then, my mind looked at the opportunity transactionally. If I helped with the bike, then he might tell me about the world outside of the ranch, something I only glimpsed on those rare and treasured trips to town or when Papa put me in a truck to go see a sale. My curiosity lay against me like a bad debt, and every chance to settle even a small portion of that account had to be taken seriously.

I told Corey to wheel the bike over to the shop, a dirt-floored building with white sides and a roof better than our house for keeping the weather off. Papa kept good machinery locked up inside. I lifted a red rock from a pile and retrieved the copper-colored key we'd hidden together. The door creaked as I slid it away. Corey watched in awe.

"You're really strong," he said, and dragged his bike inside. I felt my face grow hot.

"There's a light switch on that back bench." He flipped it, flooding the room in the fluorescent glow of a half-dozen overhead fixtures. At that time, Papa still kept the shop fairly clean. Little brown bags of rodent repellent, giving off a stench something like old insulation, dotted the outer edges of the room. Later, after it all changed, I would open the same door, and even though the bulbs above would be shattered and scattered across the floor, the light from outside would still be enough to send a hundred mice back to their holes.

For now though, everything looked the way a shop should look: slightly greasy, dust settling on some but not all surfaces, and tools in a perpetual state of semi-organization.

"Let's get the tire on first," I said confidently.

Then I began the long, arduous process of trial and error. At first I used only my hands to pull at the rubber, but one piece kept catching on a bent part of the rim. Then, fetching a pair of pliers, I made Corey hold the bike and tried to bend the aluminum into the original shape. The pliers moved, but not well enough. I made Corey hold them at an angle and hit the back with a tiny hammer. That did the trick.

Except for the fact that the tire had now come completely off the rim. Corey sat on the front tire of an International 1486 while I circled the bike. I looked up at him, and the image is so clear even today of that boy in a yellow t-shirt, mouth gaping open, a red tractor outlining his tiny frame. I couldn't help it. He looked so helpless and confused. I burst out laughing.

"What's so funny?" he demanded.

"You look funny there," I said between giggles. His face contorted in pain.

"Well, that's...why don't you just shut up," he nearly shouted. I was taken aback by the sudden shift in attitude.

"Hey, I didn't mean..."

"I don't need your help," he said, even though he had come to me in the first place. Corey marched to his bike. He kicked up the stand. A cloud of dust sailed into the air. "I'll just take my bike and go."

I had to act fast, and I knew it. I got in front of the bike, my arms spread wide. It wouldn't have made any difference. The opening of the door could have held three of me like that, fingertip to fingertip. All he had to do was go around.

Thank God in heaven, Corey stopped.

"I didn't mean you look funny...I mean... I meant it, but not like that." I took a breath. "I meant that the face you were making looked funny."

"I wasn't trying to make a face," Corey said.

"That's what made it funny," I said. "Put the bike back. You look just fine. Let me help."

He glared at me. The reality of his situation dawned on him. Here he stood, nearly four miles from home, and the bike hadn't been fixed yet. Turning it, he put the stand back down.

"I want to go pee," he said angrily and walked outside. I knew he needed a little space, and I left him alone.

Fixing the tire itself took an extra pair of hands, so I abandoned the project. Corey hadn't returned even after I squirted a liberal amount of WD-40 on the chain, so I sat on an old office chair and opened a grape Kool-Aid we had in a squat fridge in the corner.

When Corey walked back in, I showed him the chain, and he was too impressed to be angry.

"That's amazing!" he said, spinning the rear wheel while I held it off the ground.

Seeing Corey forgive. What an amazing sight. He stopped being angry so easily, so completely. I saw that, and we were friends.

4

IT IS A GENTLE NIGHT, and I sit in a dark office, the only illumination a streetlamp through my window and the glow of a Macbook. It's been nearly two and a half decades since that tire, since we worked together to get him back on the road.

I stare at the words, so small, so incapable of their dream. You on the other end read the dust, the red tractor, the buzzing lights. But how can you feel the terror at having almost lost your first friend, the quickening heart, the shaking hands missing the first several sprays of lubricant? Or how can you even see the yellow shirt, more yellow because I was young and memory can change so much?

My husband brings me a cup of coffee, and he touches my cheek. His fingers come back damp, and he gets down on his knees and takes my hands in his hands. His thumb caressed the crisscross, ugly flesh of burn scars. He looks at the last thing I've written, and he gives me a half-smile. I soften in his arms, and even then I cannot show you what it meant for a lonely child to have a friend.

I can only sit, my hands clinging to this person in front of me, and weep.

5

WE FIXED THE TIRE. I walked out of the shop, making sure to close it up just the way I had found it. The sun still hung high in the sky. I kicked a rock along the path.

"Sam?"

"Yeah?" I asked.

"What's it like living out here?"

"It's not so bad," I said. "Never lived anywhere else."

"Hmm," he said. We were approaching the edge of the driveway. Soon we would be saying goodbye.

"Do you...If I ask you a question, you have to promise not to laugh." My tiny hands formed tiny fists. "If you laugh, I'll hit you."

"I believe you," Corey said. He looked a little scared, which Papa would have called him 'sissy' for, but it just made me feel bad. "I won't laugh."

"Do you like school?" And then, in the same way it so often happened when I asked Papa a question, a million more popped into my head, each one too important to forget. I needed to get them all out. "Is your teacher a sucker? How long does it take to learn to read? Do you have a library? I saw a library once on a trip with my dad, but only the outside. Do you really get pizza every day for lunch? A kid at an auction told me that you do, but I don't know if I believe him."

Let this be a permanent testament to the patience of Corey Bruce Hoffman. He did not get on his bike as quickly as possible and pedal away. He just turned his head a little sideways and thought for a moment.

"I think it takes a while to learn to read. I can." He puffed up his chest. "A little anyway. Not as well as some of the other kids."

"Will you teach me?" I asked. I almost immediately regretted it. It was too much. Who in their right mind would commit to that, especially for someone they just met, even if they were friends now?

Corey would, of course.

"I can try," Corey said. He scratched his head. "I might not be good at it, though. I'll have to see if I can get some books from Miss Ernst. That's my teacher. She's super nice."

He turned to face me. We'd reached the end of the driveway. Both of us knew we had to separate here, but we didn't quite know how. We found something in the other that we needed, and both of us recognized it even if we didn't know how to say it.

"I'll come see you tomorrow," Corey said, and the world was alright. He rode off into the sunset in my memory, even though I know it was only early afternoon. Corey became John Wayne and Clint Eastwood, unable to be nailed down. And I remained the audience with the popcorn, knowing he'd be back.

***

HE CAME BACK the next day. I loved Corey because he accomplished something that Papa had already begun to slip up at: he did what he said he was going to do.

We hunted rattlesnakes down by the crick and over by the brown rocks in the pasture. I showed him which of our bulls had the longest horns and which heifers I named after Donald Duck's nephews. We both laughed at a dirty joke his grandmother had told him even though neither of us really got the punchline. He gave me a necklace made of an old shoelace and a coyote tooth. By the time he left, we even had a secret handshake. For the first time in my life, I had a life separate from my father's. There were now things I did without him, people I spent time with besides him. An entirely new world opened up before me.

Papa leaned on the porch railing, a cigarette gently held between pointer and index finger. He wore a tattered black stetson around the ranch. Samual Colt's pride and joy sat on his hip. He raised an eyebrow.

"Hey, Papapaul," I said.

"Who was that, Rosie?" he asked. I didn't answer for a moment. Papa's voice got louder. "I said who was that, Rosie?"

He was drunk still. That much I knew, even then. I knew what drunk was, and I knew that Papapaul got drunk often. He stood on that porch, swaying like a young willow in a gentle breeze, one steadying hand on the ramshackle railing, the other on the faux-pearl grip of a pistol. He frightened me.

"My friend," I said simply.

"He's Helen's boy?" the man slurred. A damp patch extended from his crotch to his knees and a little below. The sun beat down on us there, our own high noon at three o'clock, him an armed, drunk cowboy, me a girl shaking in her second-hand cowgirl boots. The staredown. Almost comical. Almost absurd. The first of three such instances, and the least explosive by far.

Papa grunted, farted, and wandered back inside. He called back to me, an afterthought.

"Come in and get some lunch."

***

THE DAYS GREW short. The wind became more oppressive. The cattle lowed in the field, decrying the savior's coming at last.

Every day Corey came by. We talked about when school would start up. He told me about libraries, places where hundreds of books lined shelves, each one filled with new stories. Papa had a TV, and I'd seen a library on shows, but to hear him describe it, the world had no better things to offer.

He wore three shirts, one yellow, one blue, one that was once white but now bore the eternal brown of prairie life. Dirt got into everything. Nature out there was not something to love, not really. It's beautiful, sure, in the way a hurricane is beautiful.

The weather changed, and Corey visited every day, and already I knew that when the snow did show, it would bring an ending. When you're that age, even a few months is eternity. The slow progression of the dark on the horizon each night, the quickening of winter, a bastard beast made of snow and ice, meant death to our shared moments. Surely one day I would sit on the porch from dawn until dusk, the only change a cap being unscrewed or a bathroom door being shut, and I would clench my coyote tooth, and the sun would continue its sad arc, and every moment would be agony, shivering in the Dakota cold, bundled in a million different layers stained from years of use, and even though I would want him to and I would pray to God that he would, Corey would not ride his steel bicycle up our hill and he would not great me with "hey, Rosie," so I could tell him he hadn't earned it yet and we could laugh and be young.

I was afraid of winter.

I was afraid of my father.

Then, one day, much earlier than I expected, before the first flake even fell, Corey didn't come out to our ranch. I even waited passed sunset, my lighthouse a dim halogen bulb to the right of our front door. Surely it would guide him here. Surely it would bring him back to me.

Papa came home. He'd been at a sale, and when he offered me a seat, I'd told him I was waiting for Corey. Now he pulled into the driveway. A green tractor with a cab stood proudly on his trailer. I could barely face him.

One look from my father and he knew.

"Something might have kept him, Rosie," he said in his gravel voice, and even though I was learning to be scared of him and the smell of whiskey on his breath, I ran to him. I jumped into his arms. I wept into his tattered pearl snap shirt. He brushed my hair with his gloved hand. I didn't care if he got oil in it. I didn't care that he was a drunk or that I knew he was a drunk. I cried. He held me.

I loved him. That was all.

"Let's get you some supper," he said. We made frozen pizza. Papa was the worst cook in the whole world, and he knew it, but even he could get a Totino's right. He put in one of his old John Wayne movies, The Searchers. We slept on the chair together. For that day, he was my father. For eternity, he will always have that day as my father.

***

OF COURSE, COREY had an excuse. The ridiculousness of my expectations is not lost on me now, even if it was then. He came back the next day in the early evening. I busied myself with harvesting the vegetables from a weed patch we had the audacity to call a garden. Nothing but cucumbers and three sad stalks of sweetcorn grew in the sandy soil. Corey put playing cards in the spokes of his wheels. They rattled all the way up to me. I turned to him, a too-large potato fork in my hand, the flat tines caked in dry dirt.

"Hey, Rosie," he said as if nothing were wrong.

"You don't get to call me that," I spat.

"Too soon, still?" he said, grinning.

"I waited for you last night."

"Really?"

"Really." I turned back to my pea-sized potatoes. Each had more skin than starch. My first year of gardening, and I failed miserably. My potatoes were useless. Spotted knapweed choked my squash.

I hated cucumbers. I hated Corey.

"What are we going to do today?" he asked.

"I don't know, Corey, what would you like to do?" I asked sarcastically.

"I thought we could do reading," he said. I noticed for the first time that he wore two backpacks, one gray, one pink with a white pony on the back. "I had my first day of school yesterday. I told you Miss Ernst was great."

Corey set the kickstand on his bike. His jeans caught as he got off, and he nearly tumbled to the dirt. Righting himself, he took the pink bag off and handed it to me.

"Go ahead, look inside."

I did as I was told, dropping the forgotten fork to the ground. A feeling started in my stomach. Was it excitement? Was it terror? I think both. This small parcel held the whole world. I struggled with the zipper until it came loose.

God bless Crayola. God bless Pen and Gear. And above all else, God bless Miss Ernst. She sent three notebooks, a pack of crayons, a pack of number 2 pencils with a whale pencil sharpener, an arithmetic workbook, and a book called "Buzz Says the Bee" which I still have on my shelf today. I was a stagecoach robber looking at an overflowing chest. Riches beyond imagining. Corey smiled at me.

"I would have been here yesterday, honest." He crossed his heart to make sure I got the point. "But Grandma kept me home asking me questions and making me brown hamburger until the sun went down. She's got a big church cooking thing today."

"Your grandma goes to church?" I asked. Papapaul had always said those people fit squarely in the 'suckers' category, people who talked to the air and said ghosts possessed them because a song sounded pretty. I'd never taken Grandma Helen for a sucker. She looked too mean to be one.

"Oh, she loves church. I think it's just alright, but she loves it. We go every Sunday and sit right up front." Corey picked a booger from his nose and flicked it to the ground. "What about Paul?"

"He doesn't like church," I said. The perceived slight had been forgotten. I realized I had hated my best friend for something out of his control. I knew it would be fair to apologize. I just didn't know how. "Thank you for this."

"I didn't do much except ask," Corey said. "Do you want to go over some stuff?"

I nodded. He pulled the book from the backpack.

"Ok. Can you read any of this?"

"I don't even know my letters," I admitted. Corey took a deep breath. This was going to be more difficult than he had originally thought.

"That's ok. We can learn those. He picked up the potato fork. The tip wobbled as he lifted it. Corey drew a crude 'A' in the dirt. It took all his might to do. "Here's your first one. It makes the "aa" sound. Like apple."

That's how we worked for the rest of the evening. He taught me the ABC song, which we sang to a group of disinterested cows. I knew how to draw eight letters and their sounds. When he left, I promised to practice in one of the notebooks. As soon as he'd gone, Papa walked out on the porch.

"You friends again?" he asked. I nodded. He tussled my hair. "If you're happy, I'm happy, Lemondrop."

"He's teaching me to read," I said. Paul nodded.

"If you want, we can practice," he said. His fingers drummed on his thigh as he suggested it. We both knew he couldn't teach me much. We both knew he couldn't admit it.

"If it's okay, I'd rather practice with Corey," I said. "He can't teach me the stuff you can. I want to know about tractors too."

He hugged me tight then.

See that moment. Look at him there. That was my father. He clutched me close. Here is where the weight of it struck me for the first time: a daughter needs a father, but sometimes a father needs a daughter.

When he let me go, he took my hand and we walked to the shop. That John Deere had a bad clutch, and he needed someone to hold the light.

6

WINTER WASN'T AS BAD THAT year as I thought. Papa knew what my lessons meant to me. He made a point to drive to the Service Station twice a week, me in tow, to grab breakfast.

The Bar J is one of those places that can only exist in cowboy country. Siding held to the frame of the old building, but only barely. They'd painted it white, then painted over it so many times that the paint probably had more structure than the boards beneath. In winter, the building partially faded into the landscape itself. The interior had been updated in the late sixties. Wood paneling, a tile floor, old kitchen furniture re-purposed for the restaurant. One of the chairs in the back corner was an old steel-frame lawn chair. Another was a moth-eaten recliner. Newspapers ranchers left behind covered every table. Some had been there for months. About once a year, the owner/operator would go through the whole place with a roll of paper towels and a bottle of Windex. Except for that, the place was as you found it. Grease stains. Mud on the front rug. Walls dotted with pictures of locals in various states of inebriation. A picture advertising a memorial rodeo ten years prior.

It was, in short, something in the process of dying, kept alive only by the one-handed chef who called Corey her grandson.

Grandma Helen lost her hand in a motorcycle accident. If I'd had enough experience with the outside world, I might have been afraid of her for that. The fact of the matter was that I had no outside reference. For the first five years of my life, I thought all cooks had one hand and cooked with old fry oil.

She looked the part of a woman who life had not been kind to. Lines cut across her face like rivers through a dry land. Her once-black hair now had more gray than color. Even her clothes looked beat down, dusty and showing threaded repairs at the sleeves and collar.

And of course, there were her teeth.

Yellow things, dark spots the only break in the plaque. Teeth that grinned a witchy grin. Even if my young mind could get used to much, the smell of diesel, the perpetual oil stains on my second-hand jeans, a stump hand, this was one detail even I knew to be unnatural. Rotting. Papapaul's teeth could be removed, smiling from a clear plastic cup, but they were clean. Like everything else that poor woman had, Helen's teeth were in a state of disrepair only a half-step above gone. A young girl's mind can find many things to be scared of. Helen's teeth frightened me.

Helen always smiled when Paul walked in.

"Hey, cowboy," she said, wiping her good hand on a greasy apron. A rancher in the corner snored. Every exhale sent his under-trimmed mustache trembling.

"Hey, sugar," Paul said. He always said that, followed by "Making me something sweet?"

I didn't know then what they talked about, but I do now. He set me behind a table, cracked a Coca-Cola for me on the bottle opener nailed to the sagging support post in the middle of the room.

"Why you visitin' today?" she said. Her voice had a high, hard quality to it, and an almost southern drawl even though we lived about within spitting distance of one of the northernmost states in the union. Helen fancied herself a cowgirl. Why shouldn't she? She'd ridden a horse. She'd shot a rifle. She'd lassoed a calf and shod a horse. This land had made her into the woman she was, and she carried herself like it. It wasn't confidence, not as I know it now. She didn't believe she could handle what life threw at her. She just handled it, then went back to cooking bad grits on a stove from the 1940s.

"Seems your grandson and my daughter are friends now."

"Really?" Helen said. She stepped into another room, returning with a pink lump of hamburger the size of my head.

"Seems. He's been riding his bike over to my place."

"You keeping him in line, Missy?" Helen winked at me, sharing an inside joke I didn't understand. I smiled sheepishly. Not for the first time in my life and certainly not for the last, I wished I could fade into the walls behind me. I envied water and its ability to be absorbed entirely by the dry soil.

"Oh, let her alone," Paul said. "She's shy as a field mouse."

"She'll grow out of it." Helen turned back to the stove. She dropped the burger onto the stove. Hissing and smoke filled the room. "All women do. They have to."

"Not all of 'em," Paul muttered, but Helen didn't hear him. Then, louder, "We going to talk shop?"

"After you've had a little lunch," she said. "Don't want you losing strength now." She cackled. The noise felt more suffocating than the smoke. Everything about this place was ugly, and it produced ugly things. That's what I thought then. Maybe I thought it in smaller words, or maybe I didn't think it at all so much as feel it deep down. That bright day in the fall, when the crops were nearly all out of the field and somehow we sat in a ramshackle restaurant that couldn't pass a health inspection anymore than I could fly to the moon, the weight of that desolate place settled on my little heart. It felt like wrong-ness, like life had somehow cheated us all and the only sane response was to laugh in the stench of frying cow flesh.

Paul was sleeping with her. I'm sure you know this by now. I don't know if money changed hands, but I think so.

Corey came in from the back, his winter coat undone around the collar. An orange stocking cap perched itself on his head. He saw me, his eyes darting to the tooth around my neck. Aside from our handshake, he'd never touched me before. For some reason, that day, he ran to me and pulled me into a freezing bear hug. I was so happy to see him that I even believed that the feeling I'd gotten was an abnormal thing, a cosmic mistake. Life was fine. We'd both be fine.

The lies children can believe.

Paul found an excuse to take Helen into the back room.

"Mind the hamburger," Helen said to Corey. She took Paul's hand and they disappeared up a narrow stairway at the back of the restaurant. Corey walked over to a plastic radio, something that had once been white but now looked the color of yellow sick skin, and turned on some music. He used a pliers to twist the metal peg where a knob used to be. The voice of Waylon Jennings surrounded us, but unlike the laughter or the smoke now vented through open windows or even the old rancher's snoring, this noise didn't feel oppressive.

Waylon Jennings. Waylon Fucking Jennings. Can you dig it?

He sang and we watched the hamburger. Above us, above the music, creaking noises echoed though the ancient floors. Then more human noises, distorted through wooden beams. Corey flipped a burger. We were young. We were so young for that world.

The hamburger finished, and we added thick tomatoes to white bread. The snow fell outside. Corey removed his mittens to eat. His hands were red even after this time inside. We sat and ate and pretended. The snoring and the radio and the rapid grunting crescendoing in rhythm and noise. Neither of us knew enough about the world to hold it in our hands.

7

MY BIRTHDAY IS THE DAY before New Year's. I turned eight, and I knew how to read small words. Every day I tried to learn as much as I could from Papapaul, and every evening I would study until my head hurt. I wasn't a sucker. I knew I had to work for what I wanted. And I wanted to read.

On my eighth birthday, we still had a tree up. Papa didn't do birthday and Christmas presents. Instead, on Christmas we'd have birthday cake and on my birthday we'd open presents wrapped in Frosty the Snowman or Rudolph the Red-Nosed Reindeer paper. I don't know when the tradition started, but I think it happened when I was five. He'd gotten so drunk in town the night before that I couldn't wake him until late evening Christmas day.

The Christmas a few days before eight, we'd had left-over chocolate cake from a restaurant he'd stopped at on the way back from a sale. It had been stale, with a solitary candle stuck at an off angle in the side.

Things had begun to fall apart, but not completely.

I knew my father drank, but I knew it the way any kid knows anything. I knew it was because it was, not because it *should-have-been*. Imagination is a thing used for games. Reality meant that some days Papapaul smelled like hard liquor and couldn't talk right. If you have no experience with different behavior, it's almost impossible to imagine that someone could be better.

I woke to find him already half-drunk.

I stood for a moment at the other end of the narrow hallway, staring at my father like I was seeing him for the first time. He sat with a plastic bottle of whiskey at our kitchen table, a vinyl-topped square card table with folding legs. The only other thing on the table was a two-liter of Pepsi. I rubbed the sleep from my eyes, a bit of me hoping I hadn't really woken up yet. I knew I had, though, and when my fists dropped to my sides nothing had changed. He raised a glass to me in cheers. A stupid grin spread across his face.

"There's my Lemondrop," he yelled, even though we were close and there was no one else in the house to talk over. A part of me hardened there. That yell. The solidifying of my heart. I prepared myself for the day ahead. My father drank, and I would deal with it. That was the way of things out there. That is just a sour note in the song.

He stood, nearly tripping over the wooden chair, and dispensed a kiss on my forehead. I wore pink Patrick Star pajamas. Paul patted my shoulder and got down to eye level with some effort.

"Hey. I thought that we should do something special for your birthday. What do you say?"

What did I say? His breath reeked. His eyes had already begun to look glossy. Ice coated the road. And he sulked when he didn't get his way, a pouty child who would spend the entire afternoon muttering while walking room to room in our tiny house. I said what seemed like a good idea at the time.

"I'd love that." He put a finger over his lips like we needed to keep a secret from our own walls.

"I'll go get the truck. I unhitched the trailer last night already." He stood, cursed his knees with words like 'fuck' and 'bitch'. "Get your winter clothes on. Meet me outside."

I went back to my room. A bit of rebellion or apathy kept me from changing into regular clothes. My birthday was shot. I might as well wear pajamas. I slipped navy snowpants over Patrick's many printed faces. I zipped a pink coat overtop of him and Spongebob smiling. I put on snowboots, a hat, bright mittens.

Papa honked the horn at me. I swore all by myself. Then I went out the front door and climbed in the front seat.

Papa reached forward and put a tape in our cassette player.

"I don't want to listen to music today," I said.

"You love Led Zeppelin," he reassured me with a pat on my hand. I didn't say anything else. Paul began to hum "Stairway to Heaven", then changed when he realized we were listening to "Simple Man". He couldn't even get the band right. I felt my stomach drop. Maybe he'd had more than I initially thought.

The truck rolled through our little lot. I'll give him this, even if it's not much: drunk or not, my father kept our path clear of snow those days. He may take a bottle up in the cab of our 4020, but he still got us a way out if we needed it.

"You're going to love where I'm taking you," he said. His glee might have been contagious if he hadn't hit a snowdrift on our left when he turned to look at me.

"Papa," I said tentatively. "Are you sure you can drive?"

"Course I'm sure," he said. "You worry too much, girl." He turned the music up to silence any further protests.

The drive felt like ice skating. Not the kind you see in the movies, where they hold hands in pretty little dances. Ice skating as a poor eight-year-old in ranch country knew it, the type with little to no practice. Sliding left or right across rough paths. Snow blocking one road, so a quick drift into a turn, Papa's laughing sounding suspiciously like screaming to my ears. I thought I might kiss the ground if we ever made it where we were going, but I'd put my lips on a pole once last winter and had a scab for a week, so even if we didn't die I probably wouldn't.

He drove us all the way to Lemmon, forty minutes of praying under my breath even though I didn't know God and hadn't talked to him before. He must have been listening, I think. How else could we have gotten there, enormous semi trucks barreling passed us at eighty miles an hour while my father fiddled with the knobs on the truck stereo. I still don't know how God works. I don't know why he answers some prayers and not others. I just know he answered me that day. That means I owe him one.

When we got to town, Papa sobered up his driving. I don't mean he wasn't drunk. He just rolled a window down and let the cold air focus him so that we didn't weave so much.

He drove us to a place I hadn't expected. Even if he were drunk on my birthday, the old man had a surprise or two. There, standing tall in the morning snow, iced windows glistening in the early sun, stood the greatest thing in the whole world: The Lemmon Public Library. A chance at everything I'd ever hoped for. Papa leaned back in his seat, silver flask in gloved hand, a smirk playing out across his aged face. He had me and he knew it. He'd bought me the whole earth. I could barely speak.

"You want to go inside?" he asked. I could only nod.

We stepped out into the biting wind. Papa had to grab the railing to make it up the four concrete steps, but I paid no attention. My eyes stuck to the building itself. Even the act of blinking worried me, like if I let it out of my sight for too long I would wake up back home.

Papa held the door, a gentleman's gesture. He must have seen the tears in my eyes. Leaning down, he kissed my head.

"I love you, Rosie," he said.

I loved him. God, I hated how we got here. I hate how we got there. I think of it now and my hands shake.

The library itself looked the way small-town libraries look. Steel-manufactured shelves from the 1980s in four squat rows. A reading section for little kids in one corner, the cat in the hat painted poorly over a press-board bookshelf. A quote by Mark Twain over the emergency exit. These details are how the building was, but not how I saw it. I saw opportunity. Books upon books upon books. Papa grasped my shoulder. He guided me to the front counter. The librarian busied herself in the back room. Paul rang a little bell painted like a frog. She hurried out.

Ophelia Lefevre might be the first real positive female influence in my life. She couldn't have seen thirty, but she looked wise to me in her well-kept blouse and her circular steel-framed gold glasses. Ophelia had not lived in town long, and she never told other people about her life before Lemmon. Instead, she took over the job of librarian for a woman in her late eighties and hid herself away in the squat building. She would call it a good work ethic, but any sane person knew she hid from something. I called her Opie, like the two letters after *N*. 'O' 'P'. She called me Rosie very early into our friendship, and I didn't mind.

She came out with a stack of at least ten books under her arms.

"One second," she called. It took her a minute to set them down without the tower tumbling sideways. I noticed Paul fix his hair while she did.

"Hey, there, lady," Paul said as she came to the front desk.

"Ophelia," she said. Her mouth formed a thin line. She'd dealt with cowboys before. "Can I help you, sir?"

"Business. All business. You should smile a bit. More welcoming."

Ophelia put on a forced smile. "Can I help you with something, sir?" I tugged on Papa's coat.

"Can I go look around?"

"One second," Papa said. He set his checkbook on the counter. "How much for a library card?"

"How much?" Ophelia didn't seem to understand the question.

"For my daughter. A library card," he said slowly. I, and no doubt Ophelia herself, got the impression Paul thought the librarian was a few eggs short of the full dozen.

"A library card is free, sir," Ophelia said.

"Free," Paul said. He placed his pen down deliberately. "You been talking to people in town?"

"I talk to people who come in," Ophelia said.

"They been talking about us?"

"Sir, I don't know who you are."

"We don't need charity. I can pay." Paul puffed up his chest. "I own a business, and I do just fine for myself, thank-you-kindly."

Ophelia made an 'Oh' shape with her mouth.

"I understand. No, no one has been in here talking about you two. And it's not charity. You've already paid for it. This library is run off of public funds." Paul stared at her a moment. "Taxes."

"Really?" Paul said. "I didn't know that."

"Yep. That means I can get you a card right now if you'd like."

"I don't need one. Just one for her." Paul ruffled my hair. "This is my daughter. Introduce yourself, Lemondrop."

I tried to look as professional as I could in snow pants and a second-hand coat. "I'm Samantha Rose Bauer."

"That's a lovely name," Ophelia said. She reached out and shook my mittened hand. "Call me Opie. All the other kids do."

"Do you know Corey?" I asked.

"Corey Hoffman?" I nodded, almost unseating my hat. "Corey comes in here from time to time."

I couldn't contain my excitement. I grabbed Paul's sleeve and jumped up and down.

"Corey comes here too, Papa!" I hugged him tightly. Paul laughed, a real, genuine laugh.

He stayed at the counter, signing a few papers. I couldn't wait any longer. I wandered over to the children's books. Even with my practice, I couldn't read past them yet. But as I looked over at the lines of books for grown-ups, I knew it would only be a matter of time until I graduated to those shelves.

Paul walked over to me. "Do you want to stay here a minute?"

His eyes looked out one of the windows. Ice covered it, so only the distorted reds and yellows of neon signs made it through. Across the street from the public library, a bar. My birthday present had something for everyone.

"I can sit and read," I said. I directed the second half of my sentence to the librarian. "If it's not any trouble."

"That's just fine," Ophelia said. She had sad eyes, even though her face smiled.

"Back soon," he said, and I knew he lied. I got comfortable there.

8

THERE'S A MARK FOR THAT birthday in the library. It's another cow that begins to look lean in the pasture of our relationship. Papa had taken me on trips before. But he had never left me anywhere. When we went to sales, he always kept me nearby, nervous another customer might run me over if they tried to leave too quickly.

That day, he left me with a woman neither of us had ever met.

When I wrote that last chapter, I had to get up from my computer and step out onto the balcony to have a cigarette. I couldn't stop crying. My hands shook so violently that it's a minor miracle I could even light the fucking thing. Traffic below continued onward. The one lovely, terrifying thing about living in a city is how little you matter. I wept on a plastic deck, and the taxis continued on because the world could not slow for something like my tears.

I have to tell you the rest of the story. I know that I have to. But I'm afraid to. Those two emotions of mine are dancing with each other. Fear and love, each in a waltz where they get close but never touch. He left me in a library and you need to hear about when he came back, and about how things only got worse, and about Emma, and about the day with the pistol. All of that is ahead, and I can't even get through the fucking library without breaking down.

There's only one thing that keeps me writing this damn walk through all the ugly days.

I have a child now. A baby girl. Her name is Ophelia.

9

PAPAPAUL PICKED ME UP IN worse shape than he was when we drove to town. He'd unzipped his coat and undid the top two snaps of his shirt. Gray chest hairs burst out. Red colored his cheeks. It wasn't the cold.

I sat with a copy of "The Kissing Hand" in my lap. He raised his hand in a jolly greeting.

"Ready to go, Rosie?" The librarian paused stacking the shelves.

"Hey, Mr. Bauer," Ophelia said carefully.

"There's a pretty girl," he shouted. "Don't worry, sweetheart. Don't need anything but my daughter." Paul squatted down and held out his arms as if I were a toddler walking to him for the first time.

"Do you want to go with him," Ophelia asked me. I looked at her. She had no idea what things were like. When you're little, it doesn't matter what you want. Such things are reserved only for adults, only for "real people". Children are accessories and farm hands, not creatures with their own thoughts or feelings. I held up the book in my hands.

"May I take this with me?"

"Of course," she said. Her voice became quiet. Then, a little louder, "Will you bring it back to me sometime?"

"Yep," I said, thankful for any reason to go back there. I went to Paul, and we walked out into the cold together.

"She's a sucker, Rosie," he slurred. I thought, *at least she isn't drunk*, and held my little temper. He repeated himself, louder and more forcefully. "She's a sucker. She's a sucker, working in a place like this, a pretty girl like that."

He tried several times to jam the key in the ignition. Missing a few times, he tossed them to me.

"You'll have to drive home," he said. I didn't protest. I just walked around the car so he could slide across the bench seat. If I slid the driver's seat all the way forward, I could just barely reach the pedals.

***

I GOT US home. God answered two prayers for me that day, one on the way to town, another on the way back. Maybe that used up all the credit with him because in the next years, he would be awful quiet. We drove thirty most of the way home. A minivan honked at us, but I didn't go any faster. I wish you could have seen the look on the driver's face when he passed and saw a little girl driving. I laughed so hard I made Paul stir in his seat.

After we got home, I tried to wake Papa. He wouldn't move even when I shook him. If I left him there, he'd freeze. I got out. I knew it would make him angry, so I just stared at the snow for a long time. Then, knowing there wasn't a better option, I picked up a handful. His door creaked when I opened it, but even the cold air didn't wake him. The snow down the front of his shirt did.

"What the hell, Sam?" he shouted. I'd kept it in all day. The drive there, waking up to that image of him at the card table, the hours spent in the library while he no doubt shot pool and whiskey. I shouted back.

"You wouldn't wake up!" I turned and ran inside. I don't know what he did for the twenty minutes he waited out there. I don't know if he tried to calm down, or if he cried like I did, or if he just tried to figure out what my sentence meant with so much cotton in his brain. Whatever happened then, after some time I heard our front door open and close, and then his room door do the same. Within a minute of that last door shutting, snoring echoed through our house.

***

THE SHERIFF CAME by. It was only a matter of time until he did. The next day, a knock shattered the winter silence. No actual silence filled the air. Trees always creaked. Snow always slipped from the gutters. You got used to that kind of noise. That silence was part of the song. It became a part of you. The knock, that brought something different, something unknown.

Papa didn't wake right away. I heard him stirring, but he'd take a bit to get his jeans on, then probably take longer once he realized they were going on backward. I walked down the hallway. Even our house groaned under the wind. Everything carried that weight out there.

I carried it too, I suppose.

Another knock. Polite. Three taps. Louder than previously, but not too loud.

I unlocked our deadbolt, a silly little thing, thick iron in a cheap door. I pulled the door open. There he stood.

Sheriff Coulson was a black man, one of the few in Lemmon at that time in that place. The man stood at nearly six foot four. He had a belly, but it wasn't a trucker's belly. Solid muscle hid under the fat, and not far under neither. He wore tan pants, a tan button-up shirt, a brown overcoat with a fur collar, a genuine sheriff's badge with points and everything, and he smiled easily. The smile tried to make up for his sheer size, his enormous palms, the gun at the hip. He stood casually, one arm at his left side, the other in an l-shape with a thumb hooked in his belt. The pose looked friendly. His right hand could reach for the gun easily. I stared up at him.

"Good morning," he said. Sheriff Coulson removed his orange stocking cap. He had a rich voice, all baritone and easiness.

"Good morning," I said, suddenly aware I'd answered the door in pajamas only, I shivered.

"Is your father home?"

"Yeah," I said.

"Can I come in?"

"I don't know, can you?" I said, wiggling my eyebrows. Corey had taught me to do that. Sheriff Coulson laughed.

"You're pretty smart." He crouched to my level, no easy feat. "May I please come in?"

"I'm the owner of the house," my father's voice said behind me. He stood in our living room, dressed in oil-stained jeans and a wife-beater. Paul scratched his chest. "Go to your room, Sam."

He never called me Sam. Almost never, anyways. I did as I was told.

He never told me to close my door, though. From my room, I could see Paul but not the sheriff. They spoke in tense voices.

"Something I can help you with, officer?"

"Can I come in? Have a conversation?"

"I like talking right here," Paul crossed his arms. "A little cold air is good for me."

"Suppose it's a long conversation, sir?"

"I don't expect it will be." I heard the sheriff sigh.

"No. You're right. I got a call yesterday. Someone thought they saw you driving. It was your truck, at least."

"My truck."

"Your truck. That's right. They said you'd driven a little...erratically."

It felt like even the winter silence had stopped. Paul took a deep breath.

"Erratically?"

"Yes, sir. All over the road was the exact words they used."

"I see. And you saw this?" Paul paused. An answer never came. "You didn't? So you woke me up because someone called about a pickup that might have been mine on a drive I might have taken."

"Maybe we got off on the wrong foot," Coulson said. My father spoke almost immediately, clipping the wings of the sheriff's sentence.

"No, I think it's exactly how you are." He made himself look big, and even though I could no longer see Sheriff Coulson, I knew the sight of the two of them would have been comical. My father, five six, with a diet of beer and roadside cafes, facing down an armed man nearly a foot taller. Coulson could have snapped him like a dead branch.

Instead, he said, "I'm sorry to have bothered you, then."

He left. Papa watched him go through the plastic shades.

My father rubbed his face. He turned to see me. My pale head peered from around my bedroom door. Paul sat on the armrest of our couch and beckoned me out from my hiding place. I went to him. The chill seeped into me. I grabbed a blanket from his blue recliner and wrapped myself in it.

"Come here, Sam," he said. I was afraid I was in trouble. He waved his hand at me again. "Come here, sweetheart." Papa wrapped me in a hug. He smelled awful. Two days of sweat and liquor filled my nostrils. My eyes looked over his shoulder at the mound of undone dishes. Mold crept around the edges of the bowls. Rotting milk sat dormant in plastic cups. The counter dressed itself in empty boxes of pizza or microwave dinners.

I did not live in a place for children.

My father petted my hair.

"You're alright," he said. He held me at arm's length. "You just have to know how to talk to men like that. And you don't yet. I'll teach you." He scrunched up his eyes.

"Coffee first though," he said.

10

PAPA TOOK ME TO SALES more often after that. I think back now, and I believe he was a little scared by Coulson. No lawman had stopped by before. I caught him one night on the phone. He stood in his underwear, a single bulb over our sink illuminating him. Whoever talked on the other end said something Paul didn't like. He slammed the phone onto the hook on the wall.

"I've got it under control," he muttered under his breath. I said nothing. I just crawled back under my covers.

The Department of Social Services sent a local visitor after that phone call, a bulging man who yawned a lot. He drove a Crown Victoria with fuzzy dice hanging from the mirror. When my father met him in the driveway, he didn't even get out of the car.

Paul called me over and had me recite some of the stuff I learned on the farm. The man in the car looked bored, but I wasn't fooled. This man had the power to send me away from Papapaul. I said my 'please and thank you's' and looked him in the eye and was a perfect little girl.

The man left, and I wouldn't see anyone from DSS for several years. As with others, I sometimes wonder what might have been different if that man had gotten out of the car, if he had asked the right questions, if he hadn't stuffed a Snickers bar into his gaping jaws and instead taken the time to pay attention. He didn't though. He collected his government paycheck, and as his tail lights left our property, the only thing that remained of his visit was a candy wrapper tossed from an open window.

The phone call, the sheriff's visit, the eyes in town when we went to the grocery store following us like buzzards ready to pick a dead cow clean. Paul never had a lot of schooling. He understood people, though. Their darting glances, never lingering too long lest they provoke the coyote-man to violence.

Paul looked the part, too. His hair turned more gray every day. He lost weight. He dressed in clothes washed less often. Things changed. I don't know exactly when or why, but they changed. My father's eyes didn't twinkle like they used to. They searched. They examined. He walked a slump-shoulder walk. He pawed the ground or cried to the moon before fleeing human contact.

My father was not in control, not the way he used to be.

I could only watch.

He took me out of the house to keep me from the people in town, the sheriff, the prying eyes. He locked up the ranch and the shop now, even though we never did before. Who would come looking for anything around our place?

Then came the first trip to Sioux Falls. Papa said there was a sale, and even if he was slipping, I still jumped at the chance for a day in the truck with him. We drove south along the interstate. If you drive on I-29 between the Webster Exit and Sioux Falls, you could probably stop anywhere in that whole stretch of road and see the same thing. Corn fields covered the area. Only a few lonely towns broke the landscape up. Each of these felt like islands in an ocean of snow. Paul pulled off at Watertown and drove us into a gas station.

"Hey, Lemondrop," he said. "Want to pump diesel?"

I nodded. Papa taught me all sorts of things, but for some reason or other, I'd never learned to fill a fuel tank. He showed me the screen on the pump and let me press 'pay inside'. Then he unscrewed the cap. I placed the green nozzle in the correct spot. I had to use both hands to squeeze it.

"There you go," he said, his eyes on a mother stepping out of a minivan.

We drove further. The sale was south of Sioux Falls. We'd spent so long in a car I thought I might forget what it was like to be walking again.

"Papa?"

"Yeah, girl?"

"Why are you scared of the sheriff?"

"I ain't scared of him." Paul tapped the wheel rapidly. His dictionary brain turned. "If you want to know how I feel about him, you need to know a story I got told by my momma. Your grandma." I sat up a little straighter. Conversations about my father's parents were precious gifts, given rarely and to be received with reverence.

"It's a story about a spider. The Indians called him Iktomi. Can you say that?"

"Iktomi," I echoed.

"Good. Iktomi, he's a tricky spider. And one day he sees a coyote laying down in a field. He thinks this sleeping coyote is dead, so he picks him up. Thinks he'll have a little coyote steak for supper. The coyote wakes up, but he figures 'Let's see where this goes'. So he lets the spider carry him all the way to a waiting fire. When Iktomi tries to cook our coyote, the coyote jumps from the fire, about gives the spider a heart attack, and he says 'You better make sure I'm dead first, you stupid spider', and he runs out into the night."

"Oh," I said confused. Papa heard it in my voice.

"Listen, most people hear that and they learn 'don't count your chickens before they hatch'. You know what that means?"

I nodded.

"That's not the point of the story though. The point is that if you're a coyote, you better be on the lookout for spiders who want to cook you."

"And the sheriff's the spider?"

"Damn straight," Papa said. "He's tricky as can be. And he's got a whole web of suckers ready to catch us asleep. People like that sucker from Social Services. So I just stay awake, is all."

I pondered the story for a long time. Maybe Papa was right, and you could get through life so long as you knew to be aware. Or maybe the spider should have just made the right choice and killed the damn coyote. The moral of the story lay somewhere between those two, acceptance and adaptation to the world, or being smart enough to change it. Somewhere down the road, a couple of CDs under our belt, I spoke again.

"What time does the sale start?" I asked, looking at the clock. It was already 4:00.

"Sale's tomorrow," Papa said. He smiled at me. "We're going to stay in a hotel tonight."

I'd never even been inside a hotel. I wondered for the rest of the drive what it would be like to sleep in a bed that other people slept in. Would there be clues that other people had lived there? Did people decorate it themselves? We hadn't brought any decorations, so I thought that this probably wasn't the case. But who did?

We drove into the city. Sioux Falls is by no means a metropolis today and was even less so then. If you've only ever been on the open prairie, it's the biggest city in the world. One of the most striking things was how close other cars got to each other. People wandered outside. Gas stations littered every corner. Restaurants upon restaurants lined every road. We'd come to a city of light, where neon signs flashed from hundreds of windows. It felt magical and alive.

Papa laughed. "You should see your face, Rosie."

"You should see all this," I countered. "There's so many people."

Papa drove us down Russel Street. A sports stadium, the largest building I'd ever seen in my life, went by on our right.

"What do they use that for?"

"Basketball. Football. A rodeo or two." Paul lit a cigarette. The smoke filled the cab. This reassured me. Cigarette smoke was one of his smells, a safe smell.

He stopped the truck at the Ramada Hotel. The M on the sign had gone out. When I stepped out of the truck, I nearly slipped in the slush. A man salting the sidewalk saw and chuckled. I felt my face grow hot despite the wind.

"C'mon," Papa said. The doors opened for us. A man in a green uniform stood behind the desk, reading a novel.

"Good evening," Papa said. The man held up a finger. Papa looked around. There was no one else in the lobby. The man marked his page and laid the book on the table.

"What can I help you with today, sir?"He sounded bored as if he were better than this place.

"I've got a reservation," Papa said. "Paul Bauer."

The man looked at an open maroon book for a moment. Tapping it twice, he grinned.

"I've got you right here, Mr. Bauer." He offered Papa a set of keys from a pegboard behind him. "Room 353. Take the elevator up, then go left. Can't miss it!"

"Thanks." Paul snatched the keys from the man. "Where's your shop? I need a swimsuit for her." The doorman gestured his already open novel in the direction we needed to go.

"They have a pool?" I jumped up and down. I couldn't believe my luck!

"They have a waterpark," Papa said. "You'll love it."

He took me into the small shop they had, the whole thing no bigger than our living room and packed floor to ceiling with the same type of souvenirs you can buy at a gas station. Snowglobes with Bison instead of Santa Clauses sat next to shirts that talked about why handguns are better than women. A taxidermied deer head hung on a wall. Deer heads are everywhere in that part of the world, monuments to killing. The glass eyes of the once proud buck looked so hollow to me. They shone in the yellow light of the room, and I was suddenly struck by the similarities of those deer eyes to the eyes of my father after long evenings. Then I looked to the food, saw candy bars, soda pops, cigarettes, tall boys of Busch Light. I looked out at the water park. A pirate ship with slides and gangplanks and rope ladders barely registered. Instead, my eyes went to the tiki bar. Shirtless, fat, red-bellied men guffawed in front of a line of liquor. Old women in lounging plastic chairs toasted martinis. Booze colored everything around me. It filled my vision to bursting. How many more children my age had experienced this feeling? Surely I was not the only one. I was but one of several kids all watching their father eye the same bar, watching him buy a swimsuit as fast as possible so he could turn me loose into the waiting babysitter arms of a playground or pool.

I felt sick to my stomach. Things were the way they were. That is an attitude practically bred into the people of the prairie. A cow dies, a tornado rips a barn from the foundation, a curable disease kills a man because the nearest hospital is a hundred miles away, these facts seep into the skin and bone of the people out there. Tragedy existed. What use was crying?

But I did cry. I looked on as a man ordered two more drinks for himself. I cried an ugly cry.

Paul and the cashier looked at each other, then at me. Neither knew what to do. Neither felt it was their job to do anything, deep down. Papa got down on one knee.

"What's wrong, Lemondrop?" He grabbed me by both shoulders. "What's wrong?"

How could I tell him that it was all wrong? What sympathy could he muster? I knew grown-ups. They didn't like the consequences of what they did or what they failed to do. They justified it with empty platitudes, and when that didn't work, they looked away or screwed their eyes shut like children in a thunderstorm.

"Sam, stop crying and tell me what's wrong," he commanded. I swallowed a lump in my throat. It took me a little time, but I managed to slow the weeping to an irregular sob. "What's wrong girl?"

The choice. Tell him the truth right there. It would be easy. I knew how to string the words together: *Papa, I don't like that you drink all the time.* I look at myself in my mind's eye. A red swimsuit with Hawaiian print blue flowers is clutched in my left hand. I wear a winter coat inside. I have a backpack with extra clothes in it over my right shoulder. I'd be in the second grade if I could ever just tell the man I was tired of learning on the road and I wanted to be in a real school. Maybe that little girl should have told her father the truth. But I know she couldn't tell him any more than she could tell the sun not to rise. God above, I pity that little tear-stained face, and I weep for her some nights when the moon is dark and the city is loud and lonely.

"I want a blue swimsuit," I lied. Paul looked incredulous. I knew from a young age not to be a whiner. A whiner was worse than a sucker because they made their problems everyone else's problems. Either because he was confused or he thought it was the quickest path to the barstool, he gently took the suit from my hand and exchanged it for a different one in my size. He paid the clerk, took my hand gently, and walked me to the room.

"Why don't you lay down for a bit," he said when we got there. The room had abstract paintings on the walls, all prints. Red paint covered one wall. The rest were tan. I crawled into bed wordlessly, knowing that I'd given up my chance at the waterpark with my little outburst. Papa sat on the bed next to me and rubbed my back. I pretended to fall asleep. I wanted to be alone. He waited for a few extra minutes, but not many.

I heard the door open and close. I knew where he was headed.

***

I DID GET to swim the next morning. Papa set an alarm for 6:00 AM. He needed to be at the sale, so he kept a pretty good lid on his adventures the previous night.

He woke me with a grin, and I didn't hate him anymore. Hate and love are strong at that age, but they're also fickle, as quick as a coyote and twice as skittish.

The breakfast there consisted of scrambled eggs, ham, and a sugar donut. I ate greedily. When I went to bed the night before, I'd missed supper. Paul smiled while I ate.

"Feeling better this morning?" he asked. I nodded and took a big gulp of my orange juice.

"Why don't we go to the pool? We've got about an hour and a half until we need to leave."

I left my half-eaten donut on the plate and sprinted to our hotel room.

***

COOL WATER SENT goosebumps across my skin. Unlike last night, the waterpark had few people in it. Papa sat on a chair next to an old couple. I couldn't hear most of what they spoke about. I heard him mention cows.

The couple had a grandaughter they looked after. I saw her first at the top of the pirate ship. She wore a pink swimsuit. Her eyes slanted upward, and she had the prettiest black hair in the whole world. A hand covered her eye, a mock eyepatch. When her unobscured eye landed on me, she pointed an imaginary sword at my chest.

"What's this? A rapscallion? What what? Argh, ye be a friend or foe?" The noise of the water clashed with the sound of her voice. I didn't respond, just shuffled my feet in the ankle-deep water. Chlorine smells filled my nostrils, and I wondered if the blue swimsuit actually looked better than the red one. I had no idea how to make a new friend. The only one I had had walked into my life, and he never left.

I was, quite literally, in unfamiliar waters.

What a blessing that the girl not only recognized it but that she was kind. So much can be said about human nature, and so much has been said by writers much better than myself. I have only one real insight to offer. We need kindness. It saves us.

She held up a finger with her eyepatch hand. "One second!"

I watched her hop and climb over several obstacles. She stopped only to spin the wheel once. Then she flew down the slide on the back of the boat. Water exploded around her. I ran over. She was laughing.

"That was fun! I'm Lisa. Well, actually my name is Lisha, but everyone forgets the "sh" sound."

"Which do you like more?" I asked.

"What?" she shouted over the water. I'd been whispering.

"Which do you like more?" I repeated louder.

"Oh. I like Lisha. That's what my parents named me."

"I'll call you Lisha," I said. Then, "You're really pretty."

"Thanks," she said. "I'm a pirate today. Want to come with?" She jerked her head at the boat. I nodded. We both climbed a rope ladder that hurt our hands.

"I'm already captain if that's okay." Lisha justified this quickly. "I was here first."

"That's fine by me." I shrugged my shoulders. "I don't know much about pirates.

"You be first mate. That's really good. It's the person who's in charge if the captain dies. Now, man the cannons!" I went over to the model guns and pretended to look down their sights.

"Sea monster off the..." I couldn't remember the right word for portside. "Over there!" Lisha yanked on the wheel.

"I'll get them in sight. You fire when I call out."

I stood, back rigid, waiting to hear her call. She kept the wheel spinning for a long time.

"Now. OPEN FIRE!" I pretended to light the powder and made a firing sound. Lisha jumped in the air. "DIRECT HIT!"

Then her face went slack.

"It's coming back!" She ran forward, grabbing my hand and dragging me along.

"It's got a tentacle around the ship. We need to abandon ship right now." I could see it in my imagination, towering so high it no doubt must scrape its slimy head against the steel roof. We both slid down the slide at the front of the ship. I tumbled into water that was so deep I had to stretch to touch the bottom.

I began to panic. This was too deep, and she still had my arm. Lisha pulled outward. My toes slipped and my head plunged underwater.

Papa had brought me to a waterpark. He hadn't remembered to teach me how to swim.

I flailed around. My arms swung wide. I opened my mouth. Chlorinated water rushed in. I tried to scream. Everything sounded muffled. Air. I needed air. I needed air right now I needed it now now now I needed air there was water everywhere not air I need air my hand struck something hard pain in my knuckles my feet scrape the rough bottom of the pool I needed air I couldn't fucking breathe I know fuck is a bad word but I couldn't fucking breath Oh God I couldn't fucking breath I couldn't fucking breath I couldn't...

An arm wrapped around my chest and dragged me backward. I swung my arms some more. A voice said something unintelligible. My head surfaced. My eyes stung.

Lisha had pulled me from the water. The pirate ship blocked our view of my father and her grandparents. I coughed. My lungs felt like they'd been pulverized.

"You didn't say you didn't know how to swim," she snapped. I looked at her face. She'd tried to pull me out twice. The first time I'd hit her square in the jaw. The second time she'd been able to get behind me and at least somewhat out of range of my fists. For the second time in two days, probably a record since I'd been a baby, I cried.

"I'm sorry," I said.

"You hit me," Lisha said. Her hand touched her face. "You hit me."

"I'm sorry. I'm sorry." I fell into another coughing fit. She glared at me. After a bit, she swam forward and slapped me on the back.

"You scared me," she said. "I didn't want you to get hurt."

"Thanks," I said. Lisha smiled.

"A captain looks after his first mate." She swam back towards the ship, and I walked along. "I just wish you had said something. We'll play in the shallow part from now on."

After a half hour, we'd had enough of running around or sliding down the back slide, which deposited us in much shallower water. Lisha and I sat on the deck, surrounded by the noise of rushing water. Paul and her grandparents sat fifty feet from us, neither aware that one of their kids had nearly died and the other had saved her life.

"Are they your parents?" I asked, pointing.

"Nah. They're my grandparents. My dad's mom and dad."

"Where are they? Your mom and dad?" Lisha picked at a plastic strip of the deck. She said nothing for a while.

"Where are you from?" she asked.

"I'm from Lemmon. It's a long ways away. Like eight hours away."

"That is a long ways," Lisha said. "I live here. We're just here for my birthday."

"It's your birthday?" I asked. She nodded.

"Yep. Well, yesterday was. I turned eight."

"Happy birthday," I said. A pang of jealousy sprung from my chest. On her birthday, her grandparents took her swimming. My father got the cops called on us.

"What's it like," I asked. I had never had grandparents. I suppose I could maybe count Grandma Helen, but she was Corey's grandma, and she gave me the creeps. "Living with your grandparents, I mean?"

"It's not so bad," Lisha said. "My grandma is Italian. She cooks a lot of spaghetti, which is my favorite food."

I listened to her explain her life. It was beautiful. Her little voice, which never sounds little in memory, painted a portrait of love. In my mind, she's my age. She sounds like a thirty-year-old. Even so, I imagine how she sounded, high pitched, squeaking her way through what a sleepover looked like and how she only was allowed to watch TV on Thursdays and how she always sat tall in church even though she didn't like it because her grandma had taught her how to sit like a lady.

It felt the way a baptism feels, and not because of the water.

The feeling I'd had the night before, the feeling that had been chasing me lately, the wrongness of how life kept going for Papa and I, all articulated. There was a different way things could be. There was a different life that could be lived. I'd resurfaced as a changed person. My eyes were open.

Only I didn't like what I saw.

11

I NEVER MET LISHA AGAIN. Papa called me, and I left after saying a hurried goodbye. I looked her up years later. She had a family, three kids, a loving husband, a golden retriever with fluffy fur. She ran a small cupcake shop. Nothing bad ever happened to her. Tragedy avoided her, and the world loved her smile.

That isn't the truth. You know it. I know it. The only information I found about a Lisha in Sioux Falls was a young girl who'd overdosed at a party at sixteen. The obituary said she was preceded in death by two loving parents, a baby brother, and a grandfather.

Papa drove us to the sale.

***

THE SALE HAPPENED at a nice farmhouse. That was a pleasant change of pace. Most of these things occurred at places where people had died or been in the process of dying for the last five years, leaving the grass to grow high and the buildings to lean sideways while their paint fell to the ground in chunks. This place had a house with bright siding, a new truck outside of the garage, and a mowed lawn. Papa's lip curled.

"The problem with these sales," he explained as he parked the truck. "Is that there are too many rich assholes. They get a little bit of money and they throw common sense right out the window."

I nodded. Rich asshole was just a synonym for sucker, albeit the kind who somehow had more than we did. He got out and put a cigarette in his lips. An old blue Bic flared to life. He cupped his hand around the flame. It took him one quick drag and the thing was lit.

"C'mon," he said after a few puffs.

We walked over to the food truck. They were still getting set up. The man running the grill was short and plump, with wire-framed glasses and white hair. His wife, I assumed they were married, wore a red-knitted stocking cap and a nice smile.

"Good morning," she said. Her voice sounded girlish to me, too-high pitched for a grown woman. "What can I get for you?"

"Coffee, and a hot chocolate."

"I only have coffee this morning, I'm afraid."

"Seriously?" Papa said, and I felt embarrassed.

The woman behind the counter did too. "I'm sorry."

"Two coffees." He laid a five on the counter. "Do I need to tell you how much change to get too?"

The woman took the money, handed Paul back three ones. She placed a pair of steaming Styrofoam cups on the press-board counter. Papa handed one to me.

"Do you want cream or sugar?"

"No." Papa looked at me. "Actually, yes. Two of each."

The woman handed them over. Papa took them without saying thank you. He walked us over to a trailer full of what he would call "pure shit". That was even worse than "small peanuts". Papa set the coffees down.

"Sit up there," he commanded. I climbed up next to our drinks. He opened one sugar and poured it in my cup, then one creamer and did the same. "Okay. I did one. You do one."

I did it as best I could. Only half the sugar made it in my cup, but I did better with the pack of creamer. The liquid turned a sickly white-brown. Papa nodded, pleased with me.

"Good job. Try it."

I didn't really want to, but he'd spent money on me. I took a drink. The four packets lessened but didn't overcome the bitterness. I made a little face. Still, it was warm.

"Ok. I want you to look around these trailers. If you see anything we need, let me know." With those words, he disappeared into a crowd of men his age, all lingering about the auction truck and trying to get bidder cards.

I wandered around the trailer. This sale only had two, and both had junk on them. All the farmer's well-kept tools sat in buckets or on pallets lined up before the first of the tractors. These were forgotten things, old oil cans covered in greasy dust or corded drills without the cords. I picked through a cardboard box of used spray paints. A shadow fell across me.

The man had been at other sales. His gut hung over his belt by a long ways, even covering his pelvis. He wore a shirt with a pinup girl on it that I could see through his unzipped Carhartt Coat. She rode a bomb dropped from a tiny plane at the shirt's collar. Most of the words were obscured, but even without reading them, I had a feeling they meant something lewd.

A three-day-old beard shadowed his face. His mullet couldn't save his receding hairline, which I only saw when he removed a wide-brimmed wool hat. The worst part was his smell. If he hadn't shaved in three days, he hadn't showered in three weeks. It overpowered my cold-clogged sinuses and filled me with disgust.

"Howdy," he said in a deep voice. "How're you, pretty girl?"

My skin began to crawl. I didn't want this man around me. This wasn't shyness. This was something else.

"I don't bite," he said. Tobacco juice spilled from a bulge in his lower lip. I'd never had an overactive imagination as a kid. I rarely imagined monsters or creepy crawlies. I was a brave girl.

Not then, though.

He bent down a little. The bottom of his gut peeked out as his shirt hung up around his belly button. His breath, if it was possible, was worse than his body odor. He stood in front of me. The trailer sat parked behind. He was close, closer than a man should be to a little girl.

"What's your name?"

"S-Sam," I stuttered. No one seemed to notice us.

"You like puppies, Sam?" he asked. "I got a real pretty dog back at my truck. You want to meet him?"

"Sammy!" the voice of an angel cried. Lionel, his great booming auctioneer voice carrying over the other side of the trailer like a tidal wave, grinned at me. "How are you, girl?"

The man stood up straight but made no move to fix his shirt.

"Hi, Mr. Richards," I said politely.

"Oh, now, you call me Lionel, girl," he said in a playful tone. "Come over here and tell me about life on the prairie. I've been missing stories of cowboys for a bit now."

I looked at the man, his face a mask but his upper lip quivering with rage.

"Excuse me," I said. He didn't back up.

I stepped sideways. He barely noticed. His eyes were locked with the auctioneer. Some unspoken battle occurred, one I neither understood nor cared to. Once I was out of arm's reach, I ran around to Lionel. He offered me his hand, which I grabbed.

"Let's find your daddy," he said. "I'm sure Paul's got a story or two about that ranch of yours as well, even if you are the boss."

"I'm not the boss," I laughed. My heart thumped in my chest. I knew, somehow, that this man had rescued me from something.

"Hey, Paul," Lionel said. I let go of Lionel's hand. The ground rushed by under my feet. I wrapped Papa in a hug.

"Hey, Lemondrop. Hey, what's up? Hey?" I squeezed him tighter. Lionel waited patiently. When I let go, he leaned in and whispered something to Papa. His eyes went to the immense man waddling back to his truck.

"You sure?" Papa asked quietly.

"I'm sure, Paul."

"Okay. You run him off?"

"Not yet. He's probably going back to rub one out. Creepy fuck." Lionel looked down at me. It's one of the only times I can remember him forgetting I was there. "Sorry, Sammy."

"Do as I say, not as I do," I said. Papa always said it after he talked like that. Lionel broke into an enormous grin.

"That's right. You be better than all us poor sinners, girl." He looked at Paul. "If he comes to another sale, and he will, I won't be able to get him to leave. You watch for him."

"I will," Paul said.

Lionel wandered on over to the truck the man now sat in. I don't know what he said. I don't know how he said it. All I know is that when Lionel got there he leaned in the driver's window, and when he leaned out the truck fled as if the devil and all his legions were after him. We never saw him again.

***

THE SALE GOT off to a slow start. People didn't bid much on the trailers. Papa took half of one home for $2.50 just to get on with things.

Pallets went better. We bought a small air compressor with plastic wheels and a little fuel tank. A toy pedal tractor went for five hundred dollars. I couldn't imagine what made it worth so much money. Papa told me later that the farmer's two sons were both bidding on it.

"Remember that, Rosie," he muttered to me. He pointed his coffee and index finger at one of the brothers. "Something is worth what the highest bidder will pay. That determines value. Nothing else."

I did remember that. I remember it today.

The deal though, was the Oliver.

An Oliver 80 Diesel Row Crop Tractor held a Buda-Lanova 4.9 Liter Engine. They'd been manufactured in Charles City, Iowa. According to Google searches, around 200 were made. The one we found had little paint. The seat looked rough. The gauges looked rougher. In short, it looked like a tractor that had sat in the treeline for fifteen years.

Papa bought it for a thousand dollars.

He shook as he flashed his bidder card for Lionel.

"And the old Oliver goes to bidder 137. That's right folks, bidder 137 strikes again."

With those words began the happiest days of my young life.

Papa loaded the tractor up. It didn't start, so we had to winch it on. The back tire sagged off the rim. I waited in the truck. Only once the chain binders were wrapped and the ramps up and the cursing complete did Papa allow himself to let out the giddiness he'd crammed inside.

He jumped in the cab, started the engine, and let loose an ear-splitting holler. I covered my ears. He pulled one of my hands away.

"Look, Rosie. I'm an Indian!" He slapped his hand across his mouth, whooping like some caricature in one of his cowboy movies. "I'm a Sioux Horse Thief! I'm a warrior! I got the damn thing bought!"

His enthusiasm infected me. I bounced in my cloth seat.

"Give a shout, Rosie!" I shouted. "Not enough. Give me a coyote howl." He lifted his head to the roof of the truck and howled. I howled too. His hand cranked the music loud. We rocked and rolled. We were masters of the world. We owned everything the sun fell upon. Cowboy Paul and his sidekick Rosie, lords of the sagebrush and the full moon. We had our own song of hooting and howling, and it was a life song.

"Listen here, Lemondrop," he said, turning the music back down. We'd made it off the gravel roads and back to the familiar blacktop. "That tractor ain't all that expensive. Not if you're buying or repairing. But I know someone. It's about who you know. I know a man down in Branson, Missouri. He grew up a farm kid. Then he invented some gizmo and made more money than God. He called me up one day looking for a tractor just like the one behind us now. He'll pay a pretty penny for us to deliver it to him. Hell, a lot of pretty pennies."

I took all this in. The basics of Papapaul's business model made sense to me. Buy something cheap. Sell it for more. What didn't make sense then is why the new buyer didn't just show up to the sale. I said as much.

"Because he can make more money using his time elsewhere. And he doesn't want to work. He's a sucker who wants other people to do the work. So he pays people like me, who aren't afraid of no work, and we make a killing."

"So how much is he going to pay?" I asked. Papa smiled at me. He'd wanted me to ask that question.

"I paid one thousand dollars for that there machine," Paul said. "Plus fuel. By the time we make it down to Branson, which won't be 'till after the cold leaves, I'll have about three grand into it."

Papa bit his bottom lip and shimmied his shoulders.

"He told me he'd give me fifteen thousand for a tractor like that in good shape." Papa let loose another howl. "What a fucking sucker!"

Part II

I'm just one step before losin' you.
And I'm just one step ahead of the blues.

–WILLIE NELSON

12

I COULD HARDLY WAIT FOR the snow to leave. Papa told me he'd take me to Branson, a city almost a thousand miles away. I couldn't imagine a thousand miles. My questions drove Papa nuts for three months.

"Are we going to Branson soon?"

"Couple months, Rosie."

"What's it like in Branson?"

"You'll see when we get there."

"Do you think people in Branson have ranches too?"

"Goddamnit Sam, it's six in the morning!"

Six in the morning be damned, I thought. Branson represented a chance for us. Papa and I. Here we could only be what we were. Maybe there, this other world, maybe that would be like the people in movies or in the chapter books I was just beginning to muscle through. This could be our long journey to someplace new. Neither of us would be the same after. We would come back changed, having learned some important truth about life or each other.

This transformed into a certainty in my little mind. It happened sometime about a month before the trip, though the exact moment is lost to memory. This trip took on a new life. When we left, we would leave for the better. My heart held fast to the idea of a time when Paul didn't drink. We'd walk back in the door and he'd pull the bottles from the top of the fridge and pour them down our sink. It was a childish belief.

Of course I thought it a certainty. I was a child.

One quiet April morning, before the sun stretched over the horizon, I felt a hand on my shoulder. Papapaul had his brown coat on. An unlit cigarette hung from his lip.

"Hey, Rosie. Let's get on the road somewhere, huh?" he whispered. I sat bolt upright. Papa chuckled. I sensed his muscles tensing. His hands moved to his knees as he prepared to stand. I wrapped my arms around him. He laid his chin on top of my head. "Oh, that's nice. That's real nice." He squeezed me. I was the first to let go.

"What do I need?" I asked as if I didn't have a backpack sitting in the corner of my room with all the essentials, including a book I'd borrowed from Corey rather than the library so there would be no due date to have it back and it could live next to pants and shirts for months if necessary.

"Clothes for a couple of days. Your swimsuit. Toothbrush." Paul scratched the whiskers on his chin. "Hell, Rosie, I don't know. Few days. Bring whatever you need for a few days."

At the door, he turned back. "Bring your pocket money for souvenirs."

I had a piggy bank on a shelf in my closet. I stored loose change I found, ten dollar bills deposited in Christmas cards from an uncle I'd never met, and any money I earned doing odd jobs around the ranch. Usually, Papa thought they were chores, and I did them because 'I ate supper in this house.' Every once in a while, though, he'd hand me a dollar or two after a hard day, saying nothing.

I pulled the plastic stopper from the pig and counted my money. Papa had gone outside to load the trailer. I had time, but not too much time. I decided to ignore the change that wasn't quarters, which saved me a lot of time.

I took a breath when I finished. It totaled almost $200 dollars. $174, and the pile of quarters on the carpet meant another $13. I hadn't been aware that

I'd been stockpiling for so long. My hand shook as it held the cash. They did that when I was afraid or excited, and I sure as shit wasn't afraid. I ran to the kitchen, pulled a plastic bag from the bag full of them under our sink, and sprinted back. My tiny hands shoveled the quarters into the bag. I dropped the wad of cash at the bottom. It took me two tries, but I tied the top in a knot. Looking in a tiny mirror, I crossed my heart. There would never be an opportunity like this again. I wasn't going to waste my money on little trivialities of plastic buffalo or even candy bars. With that kind of dough, I intended to buy one big thing to celebrate the trip that promised to change our lives. I swore it on our ranch and on our pickup and on the cows out back, too.

***

WE GOT ON the road just as the first rays of light climbed over the hills. I took this as a good omen. The sun rose with us. The darkness left. Surely, leaving in the early morning was good luck. It had to be.

The trip itself had the ups and downs of any road trip when you're young. I never complained. I was too afraid to. If I complained, we might turn around. Papa had never done that before, but I wasn't willing to risk it. We sang at first. I napped for a few hours. I peed in a bathroom so filthy I wanted to shower when we left. The landscape changed. I got bored. I hummed a tune badly. I tried counting trees.

We passed through a few cities. Papa bought us thick sandwiches. Mine had pickles. I hated pickles. I ate them all. No complaints. We saw a real skyscraper. Papa said we couldn't ride the elevator to the top, which bummed me out. I think he suspected I wanted to spit off of it.

We pulled into the hotel parking lot just as the sun went down. The hotel seemed as enormous as the sports stadium. People sat out on balconies, watching the sunset. Ornate trim and Greek columns dressed the exterior of it. Lights in the rock beds flickered to life. Papa rolled his suitcase behind him.

I shouldered my backpack and followed. Even though I knew it was polite to keep my mouth closed, I did my best to catch flies all the way into the lobby.

We went to a meal in the hotel restaurant. Papa swore at the prices but paid them. He left a single dollar as a tip.

The day had been long, and both of us were tired. He fell asleep first, while I lay staring at the unfamiliar ceiling. His familiar snores surrounded me. After so long, we'd made it to the Promised Land. I'd only ever prayed for Corey to come back or on my birthday drive to town. My lips moved in the night. I said thank you to God for bringing us here. I thanked him for my father. Then, whispering even though Paul was fast asleep, I asked if he might please help my mother wherever she may be.

I hoped he heard me, and that he thought it was a nice prayer, and not too demanding.

***

THE EXPERIENCE WITH the buyer could be summed up rather quickly. It took too much time.

We'd already unloaded the tractor in his enormous front yard. His house was the size of the dollar store in Lemmon. Patience, which had stayed with me all through yesterday, held on a little longer. All of us sat in a shop with a high ceiling a few feet from the house. Green toy tractors still in their boxes lined every flat surface. An old car hung high in the air on a two-post lift. Oil dripped into a rolling pan below.

Behind a steel desk with a press board top sat the buyer. Papa and I took up old office chairs that creaked under our weight.

The old, bald man in a too-tight shirt droned on about growing up on a farm. Papa knew how to handle such a man. He sat up straight, saying 'Of course,' and 'Really?' at all the right moments in the story. Paul spread the flattery like butter. The buyer ate it up greedily. He gave Paul an extra five hundred dollars for speedy delivery. I think he was just a lonely old man with too much money, so he was happy to have someone listen to him. Strangely, this is one of the few things the elderly and young children have in common: both want people to listen to them, and both learn quite quickly that people don't believe their ideas are worth wasting a pair of ears on.

I hugged him when he'd finished counting out the money to Papa.

"My dad took me here for this sale, and it's the best vacation ever," I said quickly. "Thank you."

He got down to my level. "You are sweet as a peach. You keep your old man on the straight and narrow." He winked at me.

"You've got my phone number?" Paul asked. The man pulled a red notebook from his breast pocket.

"I got my own private phone book. Your name stays in it, jockey," he said. Paul and he shook hands.

Papa got in the truck. He pointed at the glove box.

"Hand me a couple napkins, would you, girl?" I did. He dabbed his eyes and blew his nose. "Thanks."

"Are you sad," I asked. We pulled out of the man's driveway. Papa looked at the trees a long time. His voice sounded strained when he spoke.

"You know I love you, Rosie?" He asked. I nodded. "Good. Good. My dad..."

He coughed, squeezed the steering wheel until his knuckles turned white.

"I didn't have a dad. I'm learning a lot of this new." He smiled outside his mouth at me. I giggled as I always did. He popped his dentures back in. "I'm pretty old, too."

"Yeah, you are," I teased. He smiled wider. "An old man."

"Well you're a silly girl," he shot back.

"Gonna be a silly woman," I said.

"Not going to get serious on me?" he asked.

"Never," I promised.

We drove through the Missouri woods. The trip was becoming everything I knew it would be.

13

WE'VE ONLY GOT A HALF day. That's what's left of us, me and my father. We've got the riverboat forever, the eternal steamboat supper where we ate mashed potatoes and believed in second chances. That's ahead of us still.

And I don't want to write it.

I want to leave it where it sits, a happy memory in a childhood so starved of them.

I don't want to share my father with you. And why should I? He wasn't your father. He wasn't anything to you. He's just some character in your mind. You don't have the measure of him, the days he seemed to stand tall in his cowboy boots. There were days my father was a real rancher, not some words on a page. He drove cattle across the Dakota prairie. He sang a hymnal in a shop only once, and I heard it. I heard the last cowboy sing to a God he didn't believe in. You didn't. He wasn't yours. He was mine. He was mine, so why should I share him?

Why should you have the best of him? Why should you get those last times we had before it all became worse?

I know the answer. Because you've been with us so far. Because I started this, and hellfire and fury, I will see it through to the end.

Bring on the last day. See him in his bright pearl snap shirt, his hair combed back and sleek. See what he should have been.

14

WE WENT TO SILVER DOLLAR City. Everybody dressed up like mountain men or cowpokes, draping bandanas around their unshaven necks. Women wore orange tourist shirts. A marching band erupted from a bus just as we parked. Paul swore under his breath.

"Sorry, Lemondrop. Looks like we're waiting in line."

The line went surprisingly quicky. The group had pre-bought passes. Their director, a thin man who the wind would blow over if it got a little gumption to it, wrote a check. Two steel gates swung inward. The band surged through, leaving Papa, myself, and a Filipino family who spoke broken English. Papa called them a racist name when they bumped into him. The father looked at him first with anger, then with shame. There was nothing he could do in that place at that time. He could yell back, but to what purpose? No one would care. The three-toothed cashier might have even cheered my father on.

The family moved forward. Papa exchanged a joke with the cashier, the type that involves people going back where they came from. When prompted, I presented my right hand. The man behind the counter stamped an ink coin face across the back. It made me grin.

The buildings in the park looked like they were out of the 1800s. The architecture looked familiar and different to me. Lemmon had the same blocky shop fronts, the same leering cowboys leaning on posts. The fashion had changed a bit. Our men drove trucks as much as rode horses. They didn't wear so many bandanas.

A blacksmith, complete with gray shirt, brown trousers, and straining elastic suspenders, did a show for us. He placed steel in a glowing forge. While the metal cooked, he told stories and risque jokes that Papa laughed at and I understood but didn't find funny. We ate thin steaks that cost too much money. We rode rides, though not many. I was short for my age, and Papa had no real need to get on a roller-coaster. Both of us were happy enough eating overcooked popcorn out of paper sacks and watching the other people scream over the hills and around the bends of the railway system.

I hugged him twice while there. Once in front of another display, this one blown glass. It glowed bright orange. A man spun a stick attached to it, and through some magic I had yet to understand, it became a beautiful vase. I grabbed him around the midriff and squeezed.

The other happened in the gift shop. I looked at a pink purse, complete with diamond studs. These were plastic, of course. It looked pretty, and I knew I wouldn't spend my precious money on it. A feeling grew in my chest, sometime between leaving the buyer and the gift shop. The plastic bag at the bottom of my little backpack felt heavier. Its weight pulled at my shoulders. For no apparent reason, I felt more aware of the money lying in wait. There was no reason not to spend it. Instead, I put the pink purse back, some premonition telling me that there was a time very soon when I would need every dollar I had.

Papa noticed. He picked up the purse, held it up to me like some fashion mogul appraising a new product, and nodded.

"This purse suits you," he said. "Girls need a first purse." We strolled directly to the front desk. Paul wrote a check in his quick, scratchy writing. Just like that, I owned it. It was mine.

I hugged him the second time. The wind caressed the trees. Spring weather in Missouri felt warm. My heart felt full. All these fake cowboys, with their practiced smiles and dirty jokes and leaning fence posts, these men hadn't roped a calf. They hadn't faced a Dakota winter, that horrid word 'blizzard' that sounded like buzzard and meant death just the same. They were hollow echoes of a time gone by. Not my father. I had the genuine article, a real-life John Wayne. He shot revolvers and blared rock and roll. He held back the tide of progress with a rope and a whistle. The gravity of the man pulled me in. My father may have made mistakes, but he was real, and it took this fake place to make me see it.

"I've got a surprise," he said.

She waited in the harbor. She was as beautiful as the wide grasslands, taller than the rolling hills. Gray ropes kept her moored to a wide dock that four men could walk shoulder to shoulder down. In the evening sun, her white paint gleamed like the pyramids of old, a monument to human ingenuity and American engineering. It stood three stories tall, and people walked on the top deck. Two stacks billowed steam into the Missouri air. Lakewater lapped against her hull. Though she swayed a little, shallow water wouldn't get rough enough to give her any real trouble. The red paddle wheels at the back looked like they'd been plucked from the old windmills I'd seen in picture books. I had never seen a boat like her. They named her the Branson Belle. A horn echoed out over Table Rock Lake.

We strolled up the ramp, hand in hand. Riding on the Belle seemed a luxury greater than anything I'd ever experienced, before or since. Even dining in five-star restaurants or shaking hands with senators in recent years hasn't come close to the feeling. On that boat, I might have been a queen. The deck, solid beneath my feet, rumbled as the engines flared to life. Men dressed in short-sleeve shirts and funny hats called commands to one another. Ropes slithered back to the boat. Hundreds of rides in any given year had honed the sailors' skills to razor sharpness. They moved like parts of the lake itself. The current of it was their current. The pull of it was their pull. The ship backed out into open water with such gentleness one might have thought the land we left behind was the thing that moved.

Another signal horn, louder up close, broke across the lake. The wheels churned water behind us. An enormous wake extended from the ship's stern. We made for open water. Tree-covered hills passed by on our right and left. The cool water splashed upward. Green splotches of new life already appeared here, though we wouldn't see green on the prairie for another few weeks at least.

We watched a band play banjos. One man blew into an old whiskey jug. A singer with forced twang sang about a girl by the river, full of double entendres that brought raucous laughter from the crowd. I ate a cheeseburger twice as thick as my arm. My stomach bulged pleasantly. The rumble of the engines became normal to me. Everything was, as the Goldilocks story went, just right.

Rose-colored glasses. An idiom in the English language that means to look at things with optimism, a cheery outlook. It ignores the bad. It sees only the good. Some trace the origin of the phrase to mapmakers who would clean their spectacles with rose petals, something that would eventually tint the lenses towards a permanent rosy hue. To look at the past through rose-colored glasses is to ignore how things were.

Some psychologists see this as a defense mechanism, as expertly evolved as fangs on a rattlesnake. It keeps someone safe from the trampling foot of truth, so eager to disturb that which is better left alone. Truth fumbles about. It disturbs dirt. It explodes eggs. It crushes your home. How could you not want to sink teeth into that ankle?

The trip lasted another day, but that evening on the Belle was the last of the fun.

Time to take off the glasses.

15

THE HOTEL FIRST. Then the bar. Then everything else accelerating so fast you'd think someone dropped a brick on the gas pedal, oblivious or apathetic to the approaching tree.

The hotel. Paul drove through the hills. We sat content, bellies full of food and aching from laughter. Trees whizzed by. The trailer pulled lightly. The sun turned orange through the branches. Evening came upon us swiftly. By 8:00 we'd pulled into a dark parking lot. Our temporary home towered above us. I opened my door.

Papa remained still. He spun the keys on his ring. He looked like a boy who'd been caught with a frog in his pocket and didn't have a good explanation for why he'd stuffed it in his overalls.

"Papa," I said. He started. "Let's go to bed."

He smiled. It didn't reach his eyes. We walked through the empty lobby, occupied only by a mid-thirties woman watching a basketball game behind the main counter. We rode the elevator up five floors to our room. Papa opened the door for me. I walked over to my bed and laid down.

When I turned my head, he still stood in the doorway.

"What's up?" I asked. Paul stepped in but didn't shut the door.

"I'm going...out. I'm going out for a bit," he said, not meeting my eye. I knew where he intended to go, and he probably knew that I knew. We danced around it for a bit longer, neither wanting to say it out loud and somehow make it real.

"Aren't you tired?" I asked. He shook his head, still looking at his toes. All the love dissipated. He couldn't even look at me. I remember a strange combination of adult and child-like language bursting through my mind. *FUCKING SCAREDY CAT!*

He took out a cigarette, put it between his lips, then realized he was still inside.

"Fuck," he muttered, giving the smoke back to the red pack in his breast pocket.

"Would you like to watch a movie?" I tried.

"I'll be back." He opened his suitcase, placed something inside that I didn't see.

"We could watch a cowboy one. These TVs have like, a million channels. I checked."

"Probably a couple hours. No later than 11:00." He walked between our two beds and pointed at the clock. "When that says 11:00, I'll be back."

"I'm not tired either." One last desperate bid. One 'take me with you' in my protest against my own heavy eyelids. One more no.

"11:00," he said, more to himself than to me. Paul turned and left the room. Just before the end, he finally met my gaze. "Don't worry about your old man, Lemondrop. I'm a big kid." And he shut the door.

I did worry. I went out on our balcony, accompanied only by the two plastic chairs holding pools of dirty water, and watched him walk across the parking lot and into the doors of a nearby bar. I spent hours staring at the ceiling, pacing the floor, turning on movies, all trying not to worry. I tried examining every square inch of my new purse. I tried spitting off of our cold balcony. I tried praying but no words came to mind. What father should I pray to? The one a few doors down, ordering round after round, or the heavenly father who had left me in his care?

11:00 passed.

Midnight passed.

I began to really worry at 12:30. I still hadn't seen him emerge from the bar.

There was no other choice in my mind. Someone had to rescue the man. I put on my coat, my backpack, and my shoes. I spent longer than I'd like to admit deciding if a stocking cap was fashionable enough to retrieve my father from a dive bar. Eventually, warmth won out over style.

My feet carried me to the elevator, passed the now snoring lobby attendant, and out into the parking lot. I saw the bar ahead and walked at a leisurely pace. My legs hurt from all the walking we'd done that day, and from the car ride yesterday. Yesterday felt like years ago. Now encompassed everything. One foot in front of the other was everything.

I arrived at the front door of the bar at the tail end of a crowd leaving. One or two gave me an odd look, but most sauntered happily up and down the sidewalks or into the driver's seat of vehicles.

There is a place, somewhere beyond what we are. A place filled with an ocean of white flowers. It has easy, rolling hills, and fresh streams, and trees that give such wonderful shade. It holds a chance at rest, and kindness, and hope for a life that we could only dream of. I hope to meet my father there one day, completely as he should be, with all his hair, and real teeth instead of dentures, and such a smile that the shaded trees couldn't dim its brightness. I hope he's waiting for me with arms open.

I found him with arms folded beneath his head, trying to ignore the bartender. An empty glass sat next to his right hand. A long sheet of white paper lay on the other side of him. My shoes stuck to the floor as I walked in.

"C'mon, Mac, get outta here. Don't care where you go, but you can't stay here," the bartender said loudly. I walked up to the bar.

"Dad," I said. I never called him dad. He sat straight up, knocking the glass to the floor. The bartender jumped back. At first I thought the shattering had startled him. When he spoke, I realized it had actually been me.

"Jesus, Murphy, you let a fucking kid in here?" he shouted. A bald man mopping up a pile of vomit looked at him, then over at me.

"I didn't even see her, man," he shot back.

"Fucking ridiculous," the bartender said. Paul looked at me.

"Whar you doin' here, Lennondrop?" he tried, looking at me with one eye closed and the other opened too far.

"It's time to go back to the hotel," I said. I pointed at a plastic watch that had come with my Patrick Star Pajamas. The clock read 1:15 AM.

"Kid, is this your dad?" the bartender asked.

"Uh-huh," I said. "We sell tractors." He stared at me like I just spoke German.

"I'm gonna have one more," Paul told me. "Jus' one. Then straight to bed."

"We're closing," the bartender said. Dad turned his open eye to him.

"That right? I'll just..." He stood on wobbly legs. They held him up. "I'll just take my money somewhere else, then."

Paul seemed very pleased with himself. It lasted up until the end of the bartender's next sentence.

"That's fine," he said. "Right after you pay your tab."

An argument ensued. It involved trying to translate drunken slurs, only to realize those slurs were negative, followed by loud a rapping on the counter where the receipt lay. After several minutes, the heart of the issue came to light. Paul had left the majority of his money in the hotel room. He'd put it in the suitcase before he came here. Like an idiot, he had just kept ordering rounds, knowing that he could always promise to leave his license here and walk back to get it. Now he was so drunk I wasn't sure he could walk back to the hotel, much less make the trip back to the bar. He had a measly twenty-dollar bill and two nickels in his worn leather wallet. The bartender swore, then muttered something about drunks and the police.

I didn't want the cops to come. They spooked me, more than divebars or drives in winter snow. The only one I had ever really met had been run off the place by Paul as quickly as possible. I stepped forward.

"How much?" I asked. The bartender stopped jabbing a finger in Paul's face.

"What?"

"How much does he owe?"

The bartender turned his head sideways. I nodded at him, as if to say '*It's okay. You can tell me*'.

"$375." He looked at my father with such disgust. "He bought a round for the whole bar."

I looked at the long sheet. More than anything, I wanted to be home right that instant. I wanted Corey. I wanted to not be in a fucking bar.

I took my backpack off. It took me some time to dig through the clothes. The bartender tried to say something, but I held up a finger, and he fell silent. I pulled the plastic bag from the bottom and looked directly at him.

"In here is $182," I said. "It was $187, but I spent some on candy bars on the way down here even though I said I wasn't going to."

The bouncer had stopped mopping and walked over to our little crowd. He and the bartender looked at me in amazement.

"Can I leave this with you, and I promise that we'll come back tomorrow with the money?" I held out my pinky, something Corey had taught me meant a promise was serious.

The bartender stared at me a moment, then back at Paul. The bouncer slapped his shoulder.

"You should call the cops on this asshole."

"What would they do? Lock him up for the night?"

"They could call CPS," the bouncer said.

"I was a foster kid, man." The bartender looked at my father, then back at me. "She's probably better off with this fucker."

"But..."

"I'm not making that phone call," the bartender snapped. "I'm not putting a kid through that." He stared me down. "Devil you know, right?"

"Right," I said. I had no idea what he meant. I just knew that he looked like a scared deer when the bouncer mentioned 'Foster Care', and that if it could scare a big bald man with tattoos up and down his arms, it should scare me.

"I'm not taking money from a kid," the bartender said. He jabbed my father in the chest once more. "You better bring what you owe tomorrow."

He handed me the receipt.

"Can you hold on to that until he wakes up?" I nodded. It went into my plastic bag and got stuffed next to my clothes. I re-shouldered my backpack. He smiled at me sadly. "You're a good kid."

Paul glared at the man. I thought he might try to hit him. Instead, he stumbled out into the cool air. We walked next to each other, neither saying a word. Without warning, my father began to cry.

I reached up and grabbed his hand. He held mine too tightly so that it hurt. It took some prompting on my end when he wanted to sleep in the truck, but I got him up the elevator and into the bedroom. He was asleep before I shut the door.

16

THE NEXT MORNING CAME SWIFTLY. Sunshine doesn't wait for anybody. It broke through the curtains and across the floor and our faces. Papa slapped a hand over his eyes. It must have done the trick because he didn't wake. I, on the other hand, felt hungry. I got out of a bed I had barely slept in and put on fresh clothes. Briefly, at the door, I debated whether or not a kid sitting alone at a breakfast table would raise eyebrows. A grumble from my stomach settled the issue. If I could walk all the way to the bar, I could walk to the dingy room a few floors down.

They served scrambled eggs and toast. I spread two plastic grape jelly packets over a slice of stale bread. A crime show played on a television in the corner. At a table across from me, a twin brother and sister my age fought over a donut. I watched them for a moment, playing that I was at times the girl or the boy, so enamored with a pastry that it could become the biggest problem I faced. Their mother looked at me, dressed in secondhand clothes and no doubt with bags beneath my eyes, sitting alone. She had a chance at kindness, a gentle word, even a small smile.

She shushed her children and hurried them through the rest of their breakfast. It was as if I had something catching.

I woke Paul at noon. He looked over at me, then at the clock.

"Seems I overslept, Lemondrop," he said. He only looked at me out of one eye. I wondered if he was still drunk. When he stood he looked steady enough. His feet carried him into the bathroom. A loud stream of water and a sigh came from the open doorway. I knew that we would be here awhile. I turned on cartoons. The bed felt soft.

Papa took another hour and a half to have coffee and get ready for the day. He wore a baby-blue shirt, a ball cap, and dark sunglasses. By the time we got in the truck, he caught on that I was upset. I have no idea how much of the night he remembered, but he had good sense enough that morning to leave me be. We pulled out onto the road and passed the bar.

"Wait," I said. Papa looked at me.

"What?"

"We have to go back."

"Why?" he asked. "Rosie, we're already hours behind."

"You didn't pay last night," I said. I pulled the receipt from my backpack. Paul pulled off and read the receipt.

"I'm not going back," he said firmly.

"But..." I began. He shook his head.

"Girl, I know this is tough, but that man last night was a world-class sucker. He let me out without paying because he's a bad bartender. I ain't wasting my time paying what he should have collected on." He looked at me. "And he shouldn't have given that receipt to you, neither."

We drove the rest of the trip in silence. All 14 hours of it.

My father acted kinder the next few days. He knew that he'd broken something, but he didn't know how to fix it again. I had no idea either. What could be done? He wanted to go back to the way things had been. He bought me ice cream and played all of my favorite songs. The sun rose. The sun set. We ran the cattle into a new pasture. Little by little, the incident faded like an old photograph.

I saw Corey again.

It had been two weeks since our trip down south. Now even the snow around us melted off of the hills. The roads turned to mud. At a time when I wanted most to be away from my father, I found myself confined to the home place with him. He moved through the rooms like a phantom, slippered feet making little noise on linoleum or carpet. Mostly I hid in my room, nose stuck in a book I'd already finished multiple times. My heart ached for something new. If I didn't get to the library soon, I knew I would fall victim to the same cabin fever that had plagued the pirate crews of novels I'd read. Life froze up on us. I left the room to eat. Papa made half-hearted attempts at conversation before eventually retreating to his own mind when they went unanswered. Bottles came off of top shelves, emptied themselves into him, and dispensed themselves in a plastic trash can by the door. This was the state Corey found me in.

At first, he wondered if we'd even made it back. Yes, the truck sat in the driveway, but no one answered the doorbell when he rang it. Paul lay motionless in his bed, a now-dead cigarette dangling from his fingertips. I sat on my bed, a pair of hunting earmuffs drowning out Papa's snores. I might not have seen him at all. Corey had little knowledge of proper manners, though. He walked straight into my house the same way he had walked into my life. No thoughts of polite action ran through his mind.

The knock asking for entry to my bedroom, felt more than heard with my back leaned against the hollow core door, drew a curse word from my lips. I ripped the earmuffs from my head. The door swung easily, revealing Corey in his yellow shirt, hand half-cocked for another knock.

I practically tackled him.

He hugged me back, managing just barely to stay on his feet. I slapped his back with my right hand and squeezed harder.

"Hurting me," he groaned. I released him. We stared at each other for a moment. Papa's snores kept their rhythmic in and out. I wiped my eyes, aware of tears beginning to coalesce there, and mentally scolded myself. I'd become a crybaby pretty soon if I wasn't careful.

"What's up, buttercup," I said, repeating a phrase I'd heard Paul use many times. He grinned a lopsided grin. A gaping hole showed where his right canine should have been.

"Hey, Rosie!" I didn't even mind that he called me that. It seemed natural now. We were best friends, after all.

"Let's go outside," I said. The state of my house had become apparent to me, lost as I was in our initial contact. Garbage littered our living room. A half-eaten and week-old pizza sat atop our coffee table. Papa's dirty laundry hamper, overflowing with clothes, blocked the view of the TV. "We can hang in the shop."

I got us cans of Coke. We sat on old office chairs, sipping the sweet drinks. I asked Corey about the tooth.

"Happened at recess," he said. His finger found the spot where the tooth used to live. "Kinda feels funny, to be honest. Grandma Helen keeps saying it's a baby tooth, but I think I lost mine a couple of years ago, so I don't know if a new one will grow in."

"It doesn't look bad," I said. "You'll probably just have to make sure no food gets stuck there."

"Yeah. How was Branson?" he asked. I had told him all about the plans for the trip. I couldn't bear to tell him how they had played out.

"Good," I lied. "What about school?"

"School's not that fun," he said. He saw the look on my face and backpedaled. "Sometimes. Sometimes it's great."

"It's okay if you don't like it," I said. My eyes remained on my own Coke can. "I still want to go."

"Why don't you?" he asked. I forced a laugh. "I'm serious. Come to school with me."

"I can't," I said.

"Why not?" he asked. "I'm a bad teacher. But I've got a good one, and I hear next year's is good too from the older kids."

I thought about it for a bit. I stayed on the road to learn, and because I loved the scenery going by from the truck window, and because I loved to sing along to rock songs with my dad. Was this last trip a fluke? A tragic wrong note he could learn from? I hoped so. I had to hope that was all it was.

"I'll think about it," I said, and meant it. "I'd like to go back to the library soon if I can."

"It's a long ways," Corey said. I spun my chair to look at one of the tractors, a Ford 8N, which I knew for a fact ran and drove and had a full tank of fuel.

"Do you want to go for a ride?" I asked.

***

DECADES AFTER THAT day, if you ask me to describe the prairie, I'll describe it as we saw it from the steel seat of that old Ford. Corey half stood, half sat on the fender. The gravel crunched beneath our tires. Birds returned to this part of the world. Brown-breasted and chittering, they soared above us in easy formations. The brown earth stretched for miles on either side. The first planters roamed through empty sunflower fields, great disks pulled behind. A blue sky, tremendous and forever, dotted with the most beautiful clouds God ever made. Green colors returned. They started in the ditches and along the empty pastures. Cattle lowed a light accompaniment to the chugging engine. Off of our right side, a patch of purple flowers opened their faces to us.

Most important of all, my friend rode next to me. He made buffalo noises and I laughed until my stomach hurt. I told him about riverboats ten times the size of Grandma Helen's restaurant. He called me a liar until I crossed my heart. Prairie dogs greeted us from their homes on the other side of a barbed wire fence.

We'd gotten his bike to ride on the rear drawbar. It took three pieces of wire, one around each wheel and one around the seat that ran through the top link, but it rode just fine all the way to the edge of town. We parked the tractor in a ditch, I pulled the key and undid the wires. Corey had spokes on the front. I'd never ridden on anything with less than four wheels. Having already broken a rule, I found it easy to try more new things. I climbed on, and he pedaled with all his might.

It took some wheezing to get us to the blacktop. Once we hit a paved road, Corey could let up a little. We rode through the town. I told Corey where to turn. A car honked at us, and we both laughed. All the colors of the world seem brighter when you have a friend.

The library door opened for us. Opie, wearing her wire spectacles and a gray sweater, made way for both of us to walk through.

"Good morning, Sam," she said. I looked at her, then at Corey.

"You can call me Rosie if you want," I said. Ophelia smiled.

"Rosie. That's very pretty. And how are you, Corey?"

"Great," Corey huffed. His face was the color of ripe tomatoes. "Do you have a drinking fountain?"

Ophelia pointed to one. He beelined straight for it, taking in the water in loud gulps.

"What brings you two in today?"

"I'd like a new book," I said. Then, in a panic, I realized the other books still sat next to my bed at home. My ears turned the color of Corey's face. "I forgot the other books back at my house."

"Normally we have a limit to the number of books you check out," Ophelia began. She walked behind her counter. Then, looking over her glasses at me in a gesture that made her appear decades older, she said, "But I will make an exception this one time. You can check out books if you promise to bring them all back next time."

"I promise I will!" I said. I grabbed Corey's hand. For some reason, he was still at the water fountain. I drug him to the kids' section. "C'mon. You have to pick out a book too."

We spent an hour there, surrounded by all the places I hoped to go and all the people I dreamed one day to be. Oh how wonderful to spend an afternoon dreaming. Oh how wonderful to wake from such a dream to your friend telling you that yes you must go home, but he will ride with you.

I put the books in a plastic grocery bag Ophelia had behind her counter. I only took two books, one a Rhold Dahl paperback, the other a Peanuts comic book. Ophelia stopped me at the door.

"Rosie?" she said quietly.

"Yes?"

"Do you...did your father drive you here?"

"I rode bike," I said, pointing at Corey's bicycle.

"Yes. It's just...well, Corey and you both live outside of town. Quite a ways, I understand. Did..."

Corey rang the bell on his bike. "C'mon, Rosie!"

"I'll bring back the books soon!" I said. I hopped on the pegs, my right hand gripping a bag of books and the handlebars. Corey began to pedal away. Ophelia watched us leave. I know she wanted to do something. She wasn't a dumb woman. She simply had no idea what to do. Like us all, I suppose.

17

WE MADE IT BACK TO the farm before Papa had even woken up. Corey waved goodbye. I returned the wave from my front porch. He would have enough daylight to make it home. I went inside.

My living room disgusted me. These last few days told me that there would only be one person in this house capable of being an adult. I stowed my books in my room, tied my hair in a ponytail, and got to work.

My first project was the garbage. It took three black trash bags from under the sink, but I revealed many of the flat surfaces that had been completely covered. Some of the things I threw away had been lying around for months before our trip south. I even managed to keep myself from vomiting when I found an old microwave dinner by stabbing my fingertips into moldy mashed potatoes. Once the majority of the trash sat outside the house, I found some Clorox wipes under the sink. I chipped away at the dried barbecue sauce stains or mud caking the carpet.

Sometime around 4:30, Paul stepped out of his room. He looked at the semi-demolished living room and me wearing bright yellow rubber gloves. He raised an eyebrow.

"Watcha doing, Lemondrop?"

It was time for the confrontation both of us had been avoiding these two weeks. Like the cleaning, if I didn't do it, no one would.

Another standoff. The second standoff at the Bauer ranch.

"We live in a pigsty," I said firmly. First shot. Papa's eyebrows got closer.

"What was that?" he asked. His voice had dropped lower. I stood my ground.

"We live in a pigsty. You aren't cleaning up after yourself. And you aren't taking care of yourself."

"Jesus H. Christ, Rosie, a man can be a little messy in his own home."

"Three trashbags," I snapped. Second shot. The force of my voice stopped him from speaking. We never talked like this to each other. "I took out three trash bags. You need to start cleaning up your trash."

That was when he realized I wasn't mad about the cleaning.

"Look, I made a mistake, I'll admit it..."

"And the dishes." I got after him then. I really fanned the hammer. I was picking up steam. "The dishes are stacked in a mountain. You like mountain climbing?"

"Now listen..." he said loudly. He tried to dodge my rounds but he hadn't even skinned leather. Papa saw himself losing control of the conversation and he didn't like it one bit. "I say what goes on in my home."

"Do you?" I asked. "Do you say what happens?" Direct hit. A heart shot that makes the villain or the hero or whatever the fuck he was spit a little blood. He cried out like a whipped dog.

"I know, sweetheart," he said, voice trembling. There his final pistol shot, the plot twist, the bullet that cut me down too. "I'm sorry about it. Really, I am."

"Ok," I said. He sat on a chair. He looked at me then, finally. I spoke. "Ok. I'm not mad anymore."

"Yeah, you are," he said. He pulled out his cigarettes and packed the tobacco with his palm. Paul was right. I was still mad. I needed to not be mad anymore, though.

"I'll try not to be mad," I said, and meant it. He smiled a normal smile. The cigarette he pulled from the pack looked pristine against his weathered face. A white line cut across the dark wrinkles and five o'clock shadow of my father when he placed it in his mouth. He struck a match. Light flared around, then died to a dot on the end of the cancer stick.

"It looks nice," he said. I realized he meant the living room.

"We could do a bit more," I said. "But I think it looks good for tonight." Then, shuffling my feet, I said, "We could watch a movie tonight. If you wanted."

Papa took a drag of the cigarette. The paper crumpled inward a little. He wagged it up and down with his lips.

"You thinking a cartoon or a cowboy movie?" he asked.

"What do you want?"

"Dealer's choice."

I thought about it for a moment.

"Cowboy. Definitely cowboy."

***

PAPA ACTED DIFFERENTLY the next weeks. He still drank. At that point, I don't know if anything could have stopped him. But he made me apple cinnamon pancakes with lots of sprinkles three days in a row. He watched Spongebob with me in the morning and we fixed tractors in the afternoon. We talked about the flowers springing out of the ground or the rainfall we never saw. Life became an image of what it had been before, like looking through a dusty window. Parts of the glass had become discolored or blocked altogether, but you could still see the image of what we once had been.

It couldn't have lasted. Nothing does.

My father came into the house one afternoon, a laminated poster clutched in his right hand, and did a little dance at our kitchen table. He pushed the papers off to one side. The poster hung off the edge a little. I went over to see what he looked at. He raised a finger up, then placed it deliberately on a single line. In bold maroon letters, the words "HUGE ESTATE SALE!" lined the top of the page.

"We're rich, Rosie," Papa said even though the sale wasn't for another three days.

"Why?"

"This farmer bought machinery off me for years. I know for a fact that he took care of things mechanically and that he was allergic to washing things. Made him gag." Paul did another little dance. "His stuff will look all greasy, but it'll be good underneath. It'll sell cheap."

His attitude shifted. He wrung his hat in his hands a little and tried to get his hair to lay nice.

"What do you say? You want to go with?"

This was the test. The olive branch extended. He was asking a very simple question.

Is all forgiven?

I scratched my chin in a mockery of adulthood.

"I think I can make time." My father practically jumped in the air. He grabbed my two hands in his, pulling me into a dance. We spun in a circle, laughing and chanting.

"We're rich. We're rich. WE'RE RICH!"

***

THE SALE DIDN'T look like other sales. There were a few people like my father, dressed in old clothes, coats stained from years of work, smoking cheap smokes. The majority that day looked more like the lawyers I'd seen on television. Men wore long, cream-colored coats, leather gloves that didn't have cracks in them, stylish shoes not built for the mud. Papa had bought and sold machinery for the farmer, but the majority of the buyers there were his other clients, businessmen representing corporate farms or dairies that ran heads of cattle in the thousands, not the low hundreds. Standing next to such men, our song sounded hollow in our own ears. We were not rich. We could see it in the high posture, the pushed-up $300 glasses instead of Walmart readers, the glances to the few working-class folks that said more of the divide between Them and Us than words could.

Even their vehicles showed it. My father's pickup was fifteen years old and a victim of the salt South Dakota spread over its roads. Their vehicles were long black Cadillacs, brand new Fords, Chevy's with leather interiors and heated seats. Their money was a visual thing, a display for all of us poor saps who didn't have it. Papa and I were well enough off. For all his faults, he was a shrewd businessman, and his dictionary brain kept us in food and him in good whiskey. But he couldn't walk into a car dealership and drive off with a new pickup the way some people walk into a clothing store and walk out with a new shirt.

The wind tore at all our clothes, expensive or cheap.

Prairie wind at that time of the year carried topsoil. Dust surrounded us as if the 1930s had returned with righteous vengeance in its mind. Shelterbelts kept the worst of it down, but not in that open field. The nearest break was a section away, a line of sickly looking rock elm trees that could be seen groaning and bending even at this distance. Lionel had to shout into his microphone to be heard over the song.

"Forty-five, I'm at forty-five hundred need to be five thousand, five thousand, five thousand, give men five, five, five thousand, wouldyagive fifty-five, I got five on the ground gotta be fifty-five, fifty-five, fifty-five hundred," he barked. Papa spit. They were purchasing a manure spreader, and not a nice one, for the price he wanted to get some of the tractors for.

"Fucking assholes," he said. He tried a couple of times to light another smoke. More wind. The flame of his bic wouldn't last more than a moment before faltering. He cussed more. "Goddamn fucking assholes, anyway."

"On to the wagons. We're going to sell choice between the three. Okay. Let's start at a thousand. One thousand to go, one thousand," Lionel chanted. His jowls quivered in the wind.

An auctioneer, when selling an item, starts at a high bid. This number is often market value or higher. To bid on it then is foolish. After a short time, he'll drop the number to an actual start. Sometimes this is half of his first call. Sometimes it's a tenth. Whatever the case, most times he struggles running the item up to the original number, especially if it's a small thing like a couple of rusty gravity wagons.

A thousand dollars was a comically ridiculous number.

"One thousand," one of the idiot businessmen shouted, waving his yellow bidder card in the air like some overexcited schoolboy who might not have the correct answer, but sure as shit thought he did.

"One thousand," Lionel called, surprised. I'll say this for the man. Even years later, I remember him as a professional. "One thousand, now you gotta be eleven hundred."

"Yeah!" One of the ringmen, a tall, lanky boy who barely looked old enough to shave cried.

"Now twelve. Now twelve."

"Yeah," another ringman, this one just as skinny but an entire foot shorter, yelled. Soon they cried back and forth to one another. The auctioneer barely muttered numbers. He pointed his hand, and answers from the ringman switched it to the next bidder.

"Yeah!"

"Yeah!"

"Yeah!"

"Yeah!"

"Yeah!"

Both parties couldn't care less about the grain carts. I recognized it. So did Paul. So did Lionel. The bidders glared at each other rather than at the junk they bought, raising cards with middle fingers prominently displayed. It was dick measuring, plain and simple.

We stayed through the first three tractors. The bidding style didn't change. Rich men with no brains spending money like it didn't mean anything.

We went to the trailer to pay for a couple of pallets Paul had bought at the beginning of the sale.

That's where we met Emma.

The first meeting had no shadow of the role she would play in my life, nor the terror that she would come to represent. Emma looked harmless. Neither Paul nor I would have any idea how she could demolish our lives. We had no idea our world was made of glass, so we didn't even see her holding the baseball bat.

Emma carried herself with confidence. She had blonde hair that fell well below her shoulders. She strutted rather than walked. She wore low-cut shirts. If someone like Grandma Helen had seen her, she would have simply said, "She looks like a slut."

Emma sat behind a counter, reading a book that had a shirtless man on the cover. When Paul walked up, he did a double take in a move so obvious I was amazed the woman didn't call him a pervert. Instead she giggled a little high pitched giggle.

"You know you'll catch flies with your mouth open like that." Paul shut his mouth quickly. "Can I help you?"

"We're here to pay," I said after a brief, awkward silence. Papa grabbed the wallet from his back pocket without saying a word.

"What's your name?" she asked. She looked at a laptop. Back then, they were brick-like and slow. The one she had was top-of-the-line, and it still took a couple of minutes to load my father's invoice.

"I'm Paul. Paul Bauer. This is my daughter Samantha."

"Hi, Samantha," she said in that same high-pitched, girlish voice. It grated on my eardrums. "I'm Emma. You can call me EmEm. Almost like the candy!"

"Pleased to meet you," I said without much enthusiasm. We waited for her computer.

"When did you start working for Lionel?"

"About a month ago," Emma said brightly. "I'm new in the equipment world. But I've done sales before."

"Really?" Paul asked. "What did you do before?"

"Mainly car sales." Emma's computer dinged. She actually, no lie, clapped when it did. "Yay. Here you go!" She handed Paul a printed invoice. "Thirty-three dollars and eighty cents."

Paul counted out the right amount of money. He showed off the many bills in his wallet, no doubt a strategic move on his part. I watched Emma's eyes as he did. It had the effect of dangling a worm in front of a largemouth. She took the bait.

"You seem to be doing well for yourself," she said.

"Don't let the looks fool you, sweetheart," he said. "There's more to money than fancy coats." I could hear the venom dripping from his voice. Whether Emma heard it or not is irrelevant, I suppose. She either missed it or didn't care.

"Well, you just come back anytime," she said. Another awful giggle. "It was nice to meet you, Mr. Bauer." In perhaps the most unsubtle move I have ever seen a woman make, she pulled crimson lipstick from her purse and began applying it. My father smiled and strolled away from the trailer. She watched him as he went. I thought briefly that the comparison of a fish and a worm was wrong.

She looked at him the way a snake looks at a particularly fat mouse.

18

IN THE EVENINGS, IN THE now, New York sings to me. Every place has a song if you listen for it. When I first moved to a city, I couldn't believe the sheer noise. Eight million people is more than ten times the population of my home state. All of that crammed into an area of less than 200,000 acres. According to that great encyclopedia of Google, the average farm in South Dakota is 1,300 Acres. My calculator app says that just shy of 53,000 people would live on a single ranch if they were plucked up by some almighty hand and relocated.

God doesn't pick people off the street and move them, though. The people here have no idea what it feels like to stare out at the expanse in the evening, a harvest moon sailing so close to Earth you can see all the features of her face. They don't know how to break a horse. They don't know the coyote song in May. They don't know prairie fire.

I don't judge them for that, either because I have some sympathy for my now home or because I haven't gotten old enough to be bitter. Not about something as stupid as what people experience, at least.

Two days ago, I found myself in a bar. I like phrasing it like that. An accident, me being in a bar, like my feet didn't carry me there after my head made a conscious decision to go. I like the lack of accountability.

The wood of the bar itself couldn't have been in worse shape. Yellow caution tape kept one section of a counter and a gender-neutral restroom roped off.

I ordered a bourbon. It tasted so right. Here, in a place where I didn't know anyone, where the most attention I got was a leer from the fat asshole three chairs down who could have been my father, I knew that I could be Paul Bauer's daughter. I could understand what drove his mind, what drove his hands. Wore out places like this, so damaged, they feel like home because they're what I know. The lines of half-empty bottles lean like little fence posts on their angled shelf. The soda dispenser is the gun holstered. The bartender cleaning a glass is a man with false teeth checking oil on an endless line of machinery.

I felt depressed at the bar. All this writing, all this grave robbing of the past, trying to make sense of the life I once had, the life I once lived, it suffocates me. I'm trying to write you a poem about the prairie and all I can see is the librarian's glasses. Then I try to write about her smile, her kindness, and it comes out apathy. It comes out not right. The whole process feels like a bastardization of reality, or at the very least a prostitution of it.

My phone buzzed. Rupie Steinberg, a man with bright red hair in a semi-circle around his head and a figure most would call 'rotund', texted me. Rupie is my publicist. Don't worry about the description. We've been friends for years. He'll read this paragraph, call me one late evening a few beers in, and inform me I've got him all wrong, that he's much worse than I write him.

Naturally, Rupie wanted an update. There is no nice way to explain that you hadn't written in days, that you still wore fleece pajama pants even though you were in public, or that the public you happened to be in was a dive bar frequented only by those with nowhere else to go. He would have 'understood' if I told him what was going on, the way everyone 'understands' childhood trauma. What they don't wrap their mind around is the normalcy of it, the way it becomes engraved over your ribcage. No one likes it when you tell them the word trauma is for pussies and TikTok, and they like it even less when it comes from someone who's been through things objectively worse than their own experience. I once had a roommate lecture me for two hours on childhood neglect, not letting me get in a fucking word edgewise before she explained that the source of her 'trauma' was girls being mean to her in school.

At the age of her torment, I still couldn't walk without crutches. There was a partially healed bullet hole in my foot from my father's pistol.

I have a therapist, like any good millennial. His name is Bruce, the same as Corey's middle name. He smiles without his eyes, takes meticulous notes, and charges my exorbitant insurance exorbitant rates. I think I hate him.

If you read this, I don't hate you, Bruce. I just hate this fucking book, and I hate text messages from my fucking publicist. I hate that I sat at that bar drinking bourbon rather than writing the next chapter.

Rupie called. I answered.

"Hey, Sammy," he said, his tone light. It was serious. He talked too casually for it to be anything else. "How's it hanging?"

"What is it?" I asked. My buzz wouldn't get off the ground. I ordered a pair of shots for myself to help it along.

"The beta readers read the first chapter. They finished it quick, hey hey?"

"Rupe, I don't mean to be a bitch, but I'm kind of in the middle of something." Some idiot bachelorette party flooded through the front door, all pink cowboy hats and a bedazzled sash for the bride-to-be that said "COWGIRL" in rhinestone letters.

"Sounds like you're in the middle of a party," he said. I could see him in my mind's eye looking at a pocket watch. Rupert was one of those people who still owned a wind-up pocket watch in the age of the Iphone 15.

"I'm in the middle of finding out what you need," I said. The first shot was tequila. I took it without training wheels. It made me feel somehow superior in that old alcoholic way to the herd of whooping airheads. I was in a foul mood. Maybe if I wasn't a writer, I'd buy them a round and congratulate them. I just stared at them over the rim of my glass, no doubt the spitting image of my father on a Friday night, years ago and thousands of miles from here.

"Well, they got the first chapter back. They don't like the...shit, no easy way to say this." Rupert's voice sounded tinny through the little phone speaker. "They want you to lighten up."

"Lighten up," I said. Second shot. Hard whiskey. Cheap stuff that should have been mixed or watered down. "It's a memoir."

"It's a bit different from your other stuff." He was right about that. This little 'passion project' bore little resemblance to the elementary-level books about an archaeologist digging up dinosaur bones near Wall.

"Rupie, I told you what this was going into it." The fat man down from me turned his attention to the bridesmaids. My stomach turned over. He had forty years on the oldest of them. "What else did they have to say."

"Well, it's more about Jill."

Only a Jill could become the middle manager of a publishing house in New York. The rulebook pretending to be a woman no doubt had a million good market reasons for me to pack up the whole project and invent another stegosaurus dig. I don't blame her. Stegosaurus digs pay my rent.

"What about her?" I asked. I knew the answer.

"She wants you to change course." Change course was a favorite phrase of hers. Everything a maritime metaphor, and a maritime metaphor for everything.

"You're good at your job," I said. "I don't tell you that enough, you know that?"

"Come on down to my office today. Let's hash out some details."

"You really are a good publicist."

"Is everything alright, Sam?" he asked. A hint of tenderness crept into his voice.

"No, everything is not fucking alright." I hung up the phone.

Saleability. Search engine optimization. Hell, fucking web design. I didn't know what any of those things were a decade ago. I was in the middle of navigating a GED and thankful for the fact that a plane ticket to the "Big Apple" on Christmas day meant a discount.

Fatty makes a pass at the bridesmaid who looks like she has the lowest self-esteem. Her friends converge, a wall of protection against his leering, disgusting remarks. I feel bad about judging them earlier and take another drink.

Why not give up the whole thing?

That's what went through my mind in the bar that day. I was up to my knees in dirt, and if I kept digging in this grave, I was bound to be covered in it. Death smells. Old wounds leaking puss. Vindication isn't something possible for a person who's seen what I've seen, only survival. I made it out of that world, and here Rupie offered me a chance to leave it behind for good.

Tom Petty played over the jukebox. An image of a little girl, singing her heart out in a pickup truck, surrounded by cornfields, the only comfort the voice of her father sitting next to her, flashed through my mind. At the same time, the latest arrival to our empty hole in the wall. He wears a yellow hi-vis vest. Dirt stains any exposed skin. He doesn't even pull out the barstool for his son, no more than eleven. The father orders a tallboy. The boy plays a shooter game on a tablet. He is too young to vote, too young to smoke a cigarette, though he's probably snuck a few from his father's pack. He reaches up towards heaven. One day he will be a man in this damned bar. Or maybe he will escape it, and the fields will grow green, and the word forgiveness will be easy and light, and all the world will make sense.

That's not the truth. It almost never is.

I paid my ticket, rode the subway home, and sat down to write.

Part III

"You can run on for a long time, run on for a long time, run on for a long time. Sooner or later God'll cut you down.

-JOHNNY CASH

19

THE DAY OF THE FIRE, I ate Cheerios. We were well into May. Our rainfall had been dismal, even for the prairie. The thing I remember most about the days leading up to it was the cattle. We had a water pump go out on us, which wasn't surprising. The thing had been in operation since the late 1930s.

Like everything else on a ranch, the problem wasn't that it broke: it was when it broke. Heat rolled over the land like some great ancient titan. The sky in the day became all at once an enemy. It held no clouds for cover or rain. It only held the merciless sun. Driving over the reservation, My father would make countless comments on naked Indians wandering around their yards. I kept my opinions to myself. The reality was that I envied them. It looked cooler outside without clothes.

I burned my shoulders real bad the day before the fire. Corey and I went on another snake hunt. We hadn't figured out how to kill them yet, and the only one we'd seen we both were too chicken to get close to anyhow. Neither of us put on sunscreen. By one in the afternoon, both our ears were burned. He'd been smart enough to wear a long-sleeve. At the time I'd laughed at him.

Now, dressed in a tank top, my arms as red as the tractor Papa busied himself with that day, I didn't think he looked near as funny.

We went into the shop. Papa paused working on his oil change as soon as he saw me. I tried to say that Corey should be getting home, and like a dope, he said that he had plenty of time still. Papa grilled Corey for twenty minutes, asking him all kinds of questions.

"Where were you?"

"Didn't anyone tell you snakes are dangerous?"

"Why didn't you come in earlier?"

"Can't you see her arms, boy?"

I didn't mind him none. Corey couldn't tell, but I knew my father. He wasn't angry. He was scared for his little girl.

"Well, pay attention next time. I want you to take care of my daughter when you're with her," he finally snapped. Without waiting to see if the words sunk in, he retrieved a new filter and refocused on his work. Corey and I went into our living room.

The inside of our house had undergone quite the change since the last time he was inside. It took both of us working together. Papa and I kept the place neat and tidy. It wasn't an even split of labor by any means, but at least Papa helped from time to time.

We sat on an old brown couch. Corey sighed.

"Sorry about your arms," he said. He didn't meet my eye.

"It's my fault," I said. "Don't mind him. He just got spooked."

"Well sorry anyhow. I won't let it happen again." Corey's brow furrowed in a way that made his small features look very grown up. In his face, I thought I could see the man he would grow into one day. A strong jaw, a thin nose, eyebrows that only got bushier, those striking eyes that peered through things rather than just looked at them. The picture makes me very sad.

"Bad things happen, Corey," I said. I thought of a little girl without her parents, playing pirates at a waterpark. "Let's have some ice cream."

He was powerless to stop the prairie fire, though he would blame himself for my arms for a long time. Some part of Corey got hung up on my father's words. 'I want you to take care of my daughter'. Corey had turned ten a week before. He couldn't even take care of himself.

***

NO ONE KNOWS for sure how the fire started. Gabriel claimed it started on the engine of his tractor. He also smoked two packs of cigarettes a day. I had once seen him light a second by placing the burning head of the first and inhaling. I think he threw one down and the fire it started eventually consumed his ancient machine. Like many ranchers out here, he had enough to keep old equipment chugging along, not buy new. The first image I had of the prairie fire is that tractor, more brown than green, scorched, flames climbing all around the nooks and crannies.

Papa saw smoke in the early morning. Gray twilight covered the land in a blanket of false security. I can imagine him, though I never saw this, stepping out on the front porch, a t-shirt and checkered boxers, a cigarette in his right hand, a lighter in his left. The cigarette is placed in between his lips. He cups the flame. His eyes rise to the horizon, to his neighbor's ranch. He sees it. An orange glow. The sun rises in the west that morning, and he knows what that means.

"ROSIE!" His voice became granite. I sat up immediately. Papa never sounded that way. Sure he had a temper, a white-hot anger that filled the shop with shouting from time to time, but this felt different. "ROSIE GET UP!"

I jumped out of bed, threw on shoes, not even bothering with socks.

He stood in the hallway, bunny-hopping. It is the only time I've seen a man put on pants two legs at a time.

"Get water. Fridge. As many bottles as you can carry. Put them in the truck."

"What's happening," I asked. My voice quivered. He shook his head. To my knowledge, it's the only time he really yelled at me.

"Do as I fucking say, girl!" he shouted. I listened. By the time I got to the fridge, I had to wipe my eyes to see better. It grabbed the partially empty case of plastic water bottles. A few fell on the floor. I left them.

Outside, I managed to open the truck door by myself. Papa, faster than I'd ever seen him move, sprinted from the shed. He tossed me the keys.

"You remember the water truck we bought?" he asked. I nodded. Papa had bought a truck with a five hundred gallon plastic tank on the back.

"It's filling up. I need you to let it finish, then turn the water off. Then, if we need it, you're going to drive me back from Gabe's. Finish filling the water, drive the pickup out to get me. Got it?"

I looked at his old truck and then back at him. I could see the orange glow for myself now.

"What's happening," I repeated.

"Fire. A big fire." He kissed the top of my head, then got down on one knee and grabbed me by the shoulders. "That's Gabe's place. If we don't get that put out, it's going to be our place. I need you to be a big girl right now."

That was enough. I squared my shoulders a little bit and stuck out my chin. "I fill the water truck, I drive your pickup over. I can do it."

He wrapped me in a quick bear hug. "That's my girl. C'mon."

We ran to the shed together. Papa clambered up the side of a tractor.

"I'm going to get the disk and get over there. You make sure that finishes." He started the John Deere. Diesel smoke filled the room. "And you stay the fuck away from those flames, girl. You stay far away from them."

With that, he was gone. The old machine carried him back to our treeline where a disk sat. I can imagine him swearing at the old hydraulics and cursing the low speed of the machine. I never saw it.

Instead, I stood filling a yellowing plastic tank. Papa had started it perhaps ten minutes prior. It took another twenty or so to finish filling the thing. Every second felt like a pin stuck in my foot. I didn't want to stand in the shed, unable to see the sunrise, unable to see where the fire headed, but I knew to do what I was told. If I left to watch the fires progress and the hose fell out, I would be wasting precious time. Life shrunk to the sound of water pumping through a garden hose, to the buzz of fluorescent lights.

When it had finally finished, I sprinted from the shop. Halfway between it and Papa's pickup, I tripped on a shoelace I had forgotten to tie. Gravel embedded itself in my skin. I howled in pain. No one was close enough to hear it. I sat to examine my wound. Four cuts on my right knee, three on my left, and what felt like knives in at least two of the cuts. My left palm had a small gash. I decided that when the fire was out, I would complain about bad luck at length. I tied my shoe and got in the driver's seat of the truck.

The road never stretched so long. The silence of the cab never felt so deafening in my young ears. The yelling of men sounded quite like music to me. There were people working against the fire. Gabe's prairie was ahead. My father sat atop a smoking behemoth, the dirt turning beneath the two vicious rows of a tandem disk. There sat a God in heaven, and he had protected my papa. Only after seeing him did I realize how scared I'd been that last half hour. When a person is so in your life that you don't know where they stop and you start, even a short separation can become a lifetime.

Gabe Hahn had twin boys, and all three of them looked the same. They were fat men, normally seen wearing chambray shirts, with black hair and the same cowboy hat with different styles of leather ties around the crown. The father had more wrinkles and grayer, thinning hair, but the differences stopped there. His boys were named James and John, and I couldn't tell them apart if my whole life depended on it. The boys worked shirtless, their immense guts covered in sweat and soot. They lifted hoes high in the air and brought their iron faces deep into the dirt, digging a slow trench. Gabe himself fanned a cowboy hat in his face. He rode a tractor that, if it could be believed, was older and in worse shape than the burning one in the center of the field.

"Jimmy, Paul's girl is here!" Gabe shouted.

"Johny," Jimmy shouted at his brother over the roar of the two ancient tractors. The men dropped their tools and piled into the cab of the pickup.

"Go back to your place," Jimmy-or-Johnny said. I did as I was told.

"Your dad's borrowing us a tractor," the other twin said. He coughed an ugly cough. "I'm taking the tractor back. He said you knew where the key box was." I nodded. Papa kept all the machinery keys in a box on his workbench.

"Step on it," the first one said. I did. When we took the corner of our driveway, the two brothers smashed into each other, a ball of hacking coughs and swearing. I drove them right up to the shed. The tractor driver got the keys from the box. He started up a tractor, looked behind it.

"Plow or disk?"

"In the treeline," I said. I pointed in the right direction. He checked that he had a pin, nodded to himself, and drove out of the shop.

The other twin jumped in the water truck.

"Keys," he shouted. I grabbed them from the box and handed them to him. "Grab a couple of pails and get in."

Papa had a stack of old five-gallon buckets in the corner. I grabbed two of them. One had a large spider inside. I dumped it on the dirt and ran to the cab of the water truck. Jimmy-or-Johnny opened my door. The eight-ball shifter disappeared in his immense hand. The engine growled. He slammed another gear and we were off.

"When we get to the place, Johnny is going to head out for the field. The fire's about at one of our barns. We need to keep it from there." Jimmy, that was the twin in the cab, coughed again.

"Are you alright?" I asked.

"Fuck, no," he said. That was the end of the conversation.

We raced into the front yard of the home place. Out in the field, a line of fire crawled across dry grass. There had been just enough time for a little fuel to grow and then dry out that season.

"Sweet Lord Jesus," Jimmy said. He ran into the barn and came out with wire cutters. He pointed out. To the left of the fire, bare earth. To the right, fifty head of cattle pushing towards a barbed wire fence.

"Johnny'll be here soon. You start throwing buckets of water if it gets close."

Gabe's wife, a half-native woman with a toothy smile who always brought us Christmas cookies, stepped onto their front porch.

"Ma, you need to help this girl!" he turned to me. "Sam, right?" I nodded. "Ma, help Sam!"

He jumped in a small car that sagged beneath him and drove for the fenceline. I hoped he would beat the line of fire.

Then I turned that part of my brain off. I had my own fire to worry about. It came towards their barn at an alarming rate, and Johnny still wasn't back with the plow.

"Hi, Sam," Mrs. Hahn said.

"Hi," I said. I handed her a bucket. She began filling it with the spout at the back of the truck. "Not so full," I said when she had passed two-thirds. "I can't carry otherwise."

Mrs. Hahn nodded. She handed me one and started filling another. The fire grew closer.

We fought the flames, an old woman with grown sons and a girl who would be ten in six months' time. It fought back, lunging outward at us. The ground itself was our enemy, giving up its grasses to the hungry heat. I carried bucket after bucket, my arms filled with a fire of their own. My life stopped being an expansive thing, filled with reading and a love of driving and the joy of going to sales. My life transformed into turning the head of a faucet open, then closed, then waddling a bucket to throw on a section of grass, then running back to the faucet. Repetition after horrible repetition.

Johnny arrived with the tractor, ready to cut a trench with a wobbling four-bottom plow. Mrs. Hahn and I, lungs full of smoke, cheered as if our favorite football team had just scored a goal. At the same time, Jimmy's tiny car rolled through the twin trees guarding the entrance to their ranch. He gave us a thumbs up.

"Cows are out. We'll have to get them later, but they're out."

We were winning against this force of nature. A group of neighbors versus the orange death that even the old Lakota respected. Our iron horses would gallop all the way to victory. I felt like I lived in one of the John Wayne movies. In this great expanse of the west, civilization triumphed over all.

I'd heard the phrase pride comes before the fall a few times at that age. I had no clue what it meant. That day, though, I would learn.

We kept throwing buckets, now aided by Jimmy, who had retrieved a third bucket from the garage attached to his house. Mrs. Hahn took a station at the faucet. Jimmy and I cycled through. Johnny cut a trench around the east side of the fire. Then he cut one on the west. We were hemming it in. All we had to do was keep at it until the last of the fuel burned out.

I lugged an especially full bucket towards the fire. Water splashed over the rim and onto my shoes. I remember seeing that one of my laces had come untied and making a mental note to fix it as soon as I finished this trip.

You must know what happened next. You can see all the clues. The approach, the tired arms, the lift of the bucket, and the catch of the foot. No arms to steady me. The water probably saved my life, if not my skin. In all the rush and elation, I tripped into the fire.

My sunburn, still too soon to blister as it no doubt would have done, trapped heat inside. The two burns sizzled. I screamed. Dear God, how I screamed. I screamed. I kept screaming. Fire on the inside of my skin. I was so afraid. I knew I was burning to death. It hurt. It hurt. It hurt! I kept screaming. I was rolling, the world filled with bright orange, pain, it hurt, hands dragging me backward, a splash of water, someone shouting, *'Get another bucket'*, hands slapping my chest, my stomach, my back, there's dirt in my mouth, there's a pile of dirt in my fucking mouth, I can't breathe, the smell is awful, like smoke and bacon, voices, pain, arms lift me up, the sky is so blue in that moment before it's replaced by the gray headliner of a pickup truck.

"I'm getting her to the hospital," a voice says. I think it's my father.

Another voice, the deep baritone of our neighbor. "Lord God, have mercy on that little girl."

"Keep praying," my atheist father demanded. The truck begins to move.

20

I SCREAMED THE WHOLE DRIVE. The nearest clinic was in Lemmon itself. Papa couldn't hold my hand. He tried only once, and the screams got so much louder. He just laid his hand on my head. There were tears hidden beneath his voice.

"It's okay, girl. Daddy's got you. It's gonna be okay." What a ridiculous phrase when faced with the reality of pain. How could it be okay when everything felt so terrible?

He carried me inside the clinic. Nurses in blue scrubs put me on a rolling table. I writhed beneath their gloved hands. A voice behind a mask said, "Jesus Christ." I turned to face it and yelled.

Another nurse grabbed my shoulder to keep me from falling off the table. I howled and slapped at her. My other fist connected with her eye. It hurt me more than it hurt her, and I'm pretty sure it hurt her a lot.

"You've got to calm down, Rosie," Papa said.

"It hurts," I retorted.

"I know," he said.

"We need to move her. Helicopter is fifteen minutes out."

"I know it hurts, girl," Papa said. He wept as the table rolled along.

"Am I going to die?" I asked.

"No girl," Papa said firmly. He sounded like he was trying to convince himself.

"I want to!" I screamed.

"If she doesn't stop moving, we'll need her sedated," a nurse shouted.

"Stop moving, Rosie," Papa said. I screamed again. It must have looked like a scene from a horror movie, my father weeping, the scrubs turning red every time my flailing arms brushed against them, loud screams down a yellow hallway.

Someone jabbed something in my arm. The pain became less and my panic became more. I thought I was dying, and my mind tried to fight the fog. It overcame me quickly.

***

I WOKE UP in a hospital in Colorado. It wasn't much for waking up. A nurse wrapped my right arm in white. He gave me a drink of water from a styrofoam cup. I fell asleep before he had set it back down.

***

I WOKE AGAIN as I was wheeled out of the room. Papa walked next to the table, more calm now, but still worried. He wore a white t-shirt that the doctors must have given him, and still smelled like smoke.

"Hey, girl," he said.

"Hey," I said back. My voice sounded raspy. I thought about the fire. "Did we save the barn?"

"Barn's fine," Papa said. In all actuality, the barn caught about three minutes after we left. It was nothing more than a pile of ashes and an insurance check still to be cut. The wind had shifted just after they loaded me into Papa's pickup. I sighed, thankful we had at least saved it. "We're taking you to a special spot in the hospital. They've got to give you a bath."

"A bath?" I asked.

"Seems silly, right," he said. The words came pouring out of him. "Real silly. But they're doctors. Doctors have more school than I ever had, that's for sure, and these are doctors who have even more school than regular doctors. This one doc, his name is Doc Olson, he went to school for fourteen years. That's longer than you've been around, Lemondrop. Long time. He is sharp as a tack, Doc Olson. He explained it all to me. He'll be down getting everything ready. He says you ain't the worst he's seen, not by a longshot, no sir." He brushed my hair back. "You're going to like him. I know you will."

They brought me into a room that smelled vaguely of chlorine. No waterslides or pirate ships this time. Just a tub with a bunch of blue tiles surrounding it. A huge scandinavian man with a hair net to cover his red beard stood next to it.

"Good morning," he said. I wondered how it could be morning. It had almost been the afternoon when we fought the fire. Dr. Olson began to explain the pool.

They used warm water. The skin of a burn victim dies, and it can easily speed infections. Much like canning peaches, the victim is lowered into warm water and the dead skin peels easily. It floats on the surface. The whole process is disgusting. It could also save my life. The doctor asked if I had any questions.

"Will it hurt?" Dr. Olson looked at me with glistening eyes.

"It will hurt, Samantha." He said plainly. Papa was right. I liked him. So many people would have lied. Dr. Olson knew that I would know. He needed my trust, and the way to get it was the truth.

"How bad?"

"Bad. But not as bad as when you got the burns. And not as bad as it will if we leave it be."

"Okay," I said. They lowered me in.

He was right. It hurt. It would have been worse if they left me. I floated there, looking at the damage done to me. I began to cry. Dr. Olson was at my side in a second.

"Does it hurt that bad?" he asked. I shook my head no. "What is it?"

"Am I ugly now?"

He smiled at me. It was a sad smile.

"You have been one of the sweetest little girls I've ever met. How could someone like that ever be ugly?" A nurse handed him a hand mirror. "Would you like to see what you look like?"

I nodded. He showed me.

The burns traveled a few inches up my neck, but those were not bad. The worst of it was my arms, the areas I'd been sunburned and especially the parts not covered by my shirt. Both my own water bucket and the one Jimmy had thrown over me had soaked my clothes. Dr. Olson put away the mirror.

"You're going to be alright. But it's going to take some time."

21

I WENT HOME AFTER A month in the hospital. White bandages still covered my fingertips to my shoulders. Sometimes my skin ached in the night. I would cry then, softly, so as not to wake my father. He slept in a tiny chair in the corner of the room most nights we stayed there. I can't imagine what that must have done to his back. The man wasn't young, even then, and he hadn't taken the best care of himself. Papa never complained. Not once. He would greet me in the morning with "hHey, Lemondrop," and send me to sleep with an "I know tomorrow will be even better." He pushed my wheelchair out the hospital doors.

The drive back to the ranch had that comforting feeling of going home mixed with the anxiety of knowing you had changed. Gabe had driven Papa's truck out to us and cared for the cows while we waited to be dismissed. He told Papa that it was the least he could do. They spoke in a narrow hallway just outside my room's door. He wouldn't, or maybe couldn't, come in.

I glanced at my face in the rearview mirror. Inside I thought of myself the same. Outside, I couldn't help but think of the raw pink flesh hiding beneath cloth wraps. I looked monstrous, like something out of a late-night scary movie, the type that always made me change the channel as fast as my fingers could press the button.

Papa pulled a cassette tape from a box under his seat.

"Who'd you pick?" I asked.

"You'll see," he said. The familiar bump and swing filled our truck. A twang of a guitar joined in.

***

I WOKE THAT first night back. I stared at the walls of my room, so foreign even though it had been just a short while ago they meant familiarity. Eventually I gave up on getting back to sleep. I wandered out our back door. An old swingset, really just a few iron bars that should have been torn down years ago, leaned left in the light of a crescent moon. I sat on the swing. Metal groaned beneath my weight.

New York City, I've learned, has lights and noise, and there can be a tremendous community in a place that treats sleep like a stranger. There's a unique experience to stargazing on the prairie, though. No amount of neon can compare to the glistening dots covering the sky, the arm of the Milky Way purple-pink cutting through the black. On that night, bright lights lit the sky, great waves of green pulsating around the stars.

"Aurora Borealis." My father's voice made me jump. He had a blanket around his shoulders and a quilt my grandmother made in his hands. He draped this over me, tucking in my shoulders with gentle hands. I winced, but only a little. "Northern lights. People think it happens because of magnets."

"Like on our fridge?" I asked. I thought he was telling a tall tale.

"Not quite," he chuckled. "They say it's properties of iron in the dirt."

"I don't think so," I said.

"Me neither," Papa said. We stared at the sky.

"What do you think causes it?"

"I don't know. I think we don't need to know for sure about everything." He lit a smoke. The smell calmed me. Cigarettes were a staple of my childhood. They smelled like people who cared about me. "I heard a story about it, once."

"The lights?"

"Yep. An old Indian told it to me," he said. I narrowed my eyes. "Honest. Not made up. He sat next to me in a bar out near Wall. According to him, the lights happened because the buffalo left this land. The tribe sent some bowlegged young buck after him. This young kid, he's wet behind the ears." Here he tickled me behind my ears. I laughed. "But he was a good tracker. Best tracker in the whole tribe. He follows the buffalo way up north. All the way into Canada, and out west where tall mountains grow like grass. He follows tracks up the tallest mountain, and he knows he's going to find what he needs to find at the top. He climbs over rocks and across trails, following the deep buffalo footprints, all the way to the mountain peak and..."

He paused for dramatic effect. I leaned in. Paul's voice was a whisper. "No buffalo."

"What do you mean, no buffalo?" I demanded. "That's no way to end a story."

"I'm getting there. Hold your horses." He puffed a large cloud. "Buffalo herd had galloped right into the sky. The lights, they're the buffalo fathers, all trampling and snorting and starlight. And here, the man at the bar, he leans in real close. I can smell the liquor on his breath. He grabs my shoulder, and he says 'They'll come back to us, one day. I know it.'" Papa stared up at the lights for a long time. His fingers played with the top snap of his shirt. "Must've been strange for him, feeling like the whole world had moved on to a new time."

He was trying to tell me something about himself. I couldn't figure out what, though.

"Come on," he said. "Lights are pretty, but you need rest. Come on, now."

We went inside together.

***

COREY AND GRANDMA Helen drove out the next day. I didn't even realize Helen had a car, though that was probably a generous thing to call the box of rust and black smoke-spewing engine. They roared up our driveway, the little Pontiac louder than Papa's truck. Helen hadn't even brought the car to a full stop before Corey was out and running. He slowed when he got close to me. I looked at him, his stupid yellow t-shirt, his blonde hair almost shoulder length, his eyes that saw more than mine on all of our snakehunts and hangouts, and I was afraid. I had bandages, a pale face, greasy hair. I knew he would laugh at me.

He hugged me so tightly I thought I might burst. My burns screamed at his touch. He released me quickly.

"I was so scared," he said. His voice cracked. "Don't ever do that again. Don't you ever get hurt again. It hurt me that you got hurt." He cried. My father, in other circumstances, would have called him a sissy boy for that. Not today. Today he cried and no one said a word about it.

"I didn't mean to," I said, my own face now a mess of tears.

"I know," Corey said. "I just got so scared. I wanted to visit in the hospital." He looked at the car. It had made it here, and that impressed me. A trip to Colorado would have been unthinkable.

"I'm glad you're feeling better," Helen said in her high, hard voice. She smiled a terrible smile at me, then actually kissed my forehead. She smelled like fry oil and salt. "I was so worried about you, girl."

"Thanks," I said. Until then, I had never considered myself someone Helen really noticed, let alone became fond of.

"Hey, Helen," my father said, giving her a peck on the cheek. "How are you?"

"Same old, same old, cowboy," she said. "Oh, I almost forgot." She went to the car and retrieved a rectangular steel baking pan. White frosting covered the top. "Carrot cake!"

The cake itself had a sickly orange color, but it tasted divine. Corey and I had two pieces each. After, Papa said he needed to discuss business with Helen, and told us to go hunt down some trouble.

"Be careful," he said. I nodded.

Corey and I didn't find any trouble, just some cows. We kicked rocks up the road, saying very little until the house became a tiny model in the distance.

"I think you should go to school with me," Corey said suddenly. I faced him. He shook a little, but his face was firm. "I know you love your dad. But I think you should go to school with me."

"I learn on the road," I said.

"Do you want to?" he asked. I didn't answer. "You said you would think about it."

That seemed to happen to another person. A few months, that was all that separated our tractor ride to the library and now. How could it seem years had passed? Time felt infinite at that age. Everything happened slower.

"I just don't know."

"We start in August. That's not far off. Come with." Corey looked down at his hands. "I want you to go with."

I did too. I realized that I couldn't ignore what I wanted anymore. I had been following around my father, sale to sale, state to state, and I was tired. I wanted to learn math without tractors and reading without long trips to the town library. Most of all, I wanted to see Corey more. Sometimes we went over a week without each other. The time in the hospital hadn't just been hard on him. I had felt lonesome, laid up in a bed and unable to talk about horseback riding or try to find wildflowers.

In the distance, up the road, a cop car turned onto our gravel driveway. Corey and I ran back to the house.

22

PAPA GOT DRESSED QUICKLY WHEN he heard the sheriff was on the way. He looked at Helen.

"You should probably go," he said. Helen shook her head.

"I'll fix up some lunch. You and the lawman can talk in the kitchen."

"You're a blessing," Paul said. He looked at Corey and I. "Go play out back. Keep your noses out of this, you hear?" We both nodded. I led him around the back of the house. We started by kicking a ball around. The sound of tires on gravel, of a car door opening and shutting, reached us. Fragments of a conversation at the front door followed.

"I need to listen," I told Corey. His eyes widened.

"But Paul said..."

"I need to listen," I repeated. "Are you coming with?" He swallowed, then nodded. We crept towards the house. Grandma Helen had opened the kitchen window to vent smoke outside. The entire conversation was punctuated with the sound and smell of frying bacon.

"Thank you for inviting me in," the baritone of the sheriff said. Corey and I stood flat against the building. Helen would have to stick her whole head out the window to see us. She'd sooner believe we went to a tree grove out back than listen in anyway.

"What can I do you for?" Paul asked.

"I'm just passing through."

"Passing through?"

"That's right," Sheriff Coulson said. I pictured him leaning back in his chair, his brown eyes scanning the room around him. They would move slowly, lethargically, his intent hidden beneath the slothful movement. Papa wouldn't be fooled. The man would be looking for evidence of a crime. "I've been hearing stories in town."

"People talk too much nowadays," Papa said. I pictured him as well, cool, collected, the smell of Helen still clinging to him. "So many words and nothing to say."

"Mmm," Coulson agreed. "Can I smoke here?"

"I ain't gonna stop you."

"Thanks." A lull. The immense man lighting a tiny cigarette. My father lighting his own.

"You like lettuce and tomato?" Helen interrupted.

"If it's not too much trouble," Coulson said. Two plates clattered onto our kitchen card table. I felt sick to my stomach. Every sentence the sheriff said just sounded like a rattle to me. "Heard you had a little visit to the hospital?"

"I did," Papa said.

"Mmm. Long time out there. What was that all about?"

"You just prying?"

Coulson paused for a moment. His face in my mind grew serious. Cold. "Making conversation."

"Tough to talk about."

"Mmm. I bet. And I don't want to pry. How about we talk about that adorable girl of yours? She's what, five?"

"Nine," Papa said, his voice a knife.

"Nine. I looked around, just curious. I don't see her registered for school anywhere?"

"My little girl is smarter than any other kid her age." Papa puffed with pride. "She can calculate advanced transactions in her head. A human calculator, that girl."

"Mmm. Mmm."

"Sheriff, you haven't touched your sandwich," Helen cut in.

"He's fine, Helen," Paul said quietly. "He'll eat if he's hungry."

"I did have a big meal before here," Coulson said. "I've got to try it though."

Another break, filled only with bacon sizzle and chewing.

"So these...well-meaning folks, the chatty ones..." Paul began.

"Excellent tomatoes. Pardon my swearing, but a damn good sandwich."

"These people," Paul tried again. "What have they been saying?"

Sheriff Coulson spoke with his mouth full. "They've been saying that you went to take Samantha to the hospital. That she got burned up pretty bad. Hurt her a lot."

"She's tough," Paul interjected.

"That's also what I heard. Just talk, all of it. I wanted to come by and see how she was doing."

"She's out back with Helen's boy. Doing fine. Real fine."

"That's good." Coulson took a gulp of water so loud we heard it from outside. "I think that you've got a fine place here. Plenty of room for a kid to be a kid. I wonder, though, if it isn't a little less structured than a growing person needs."

"You questioning my parenting?" Paul said quietly. There was a hammer drawing back in those words, in the easy delivery, the soft consonants.

"Absolutely not," Coulson responded. "I'd hate to offend. Like you said. A lot of talk. Probably nothing to say."

The dishes were cleared. The two men sat across from each other, finishing cigarettes.

"I'd like to talk to Samantha, if you're okay with it."

"Why?" Paul demanded.

"See how she's feeling."

"I said she's fine."

"I know. Call it an unfortunate part of the job. People say a girl is burned, a girl who should be school age, she spends a month out of town, I wouldn't be a cop if I left with a 'she feels fine'. I got to hear it from the horse's mouth, so to speak."

"What if I tell you to get the hell off my land," Paul asked.

"That'd be concerning. I haven't even seen the girl back here. No real way to confirm she made it home. No witnesses except I assume you, ma'am," Coulson said, addressing Helen for the first time. "No sir, I think we'd both be happier if I can leave here and write that everything is normal on the Bauer Ranch."

"I'll get her." A chair pushed away from the table. "And you can still go to hell. Before or after your little chat, makes no difference to me."

***

THE KITCHEN FELT off to me that day. My father stood behind Sheriff Coulson. The officer sat in one of the four metal folding chairs around our card table. The remnants of his small meal had disappeared into the kitchen. Paul seemed too small in that room. The silence seemed so large. Corey leaned in the doorway. A tattered screen door rested against his back. I swallowed.

"Hey, Samantha. Do you remember me?" Sheriff Coulson asked. I nodded.

"I heard you had a visit to the hospital. How are you?"

"Good." My voice sounded strained. The pain in my arms, an ever-present undercurrent for the past month, rose to the top. It demanded attention. I didn't want foster care. I didn't want to talk to this man. I wanted him to go away so I could hunt snakes with my friend and eat french fries cooked in too much oil. Grandma Helen, my father, Corey, these people belonged in our tiny house. The officer with massive shoulders, a pleasant, forced smile, a gun on his hip, he had no place here.

"Do you want something to eat?" Grandma Helen asked.

"No, thank you," I said.

"Good manners," Sheriff Coulson said. He nodded to himself. The air suffocated me. Bacon haze encompassed our meeting. Years later, when I sat in a college dorm after a particularly dull creative writing class, my roommate would teach me how to play chess. The game would remind me of this day, this conversation.

Opening move.

"Why don't you sit down for a bit?" Sheriff Coulson asked. We both knew that it wasn't the type of question I could refuse. Manners were a smokescreen here. He was an adult and a servant of the law. I was just me. I sat. He produced a small red-covered notepad and pen from his breast pocket. "There's no need to be nervous. I just want to ask a couple of questions."

"Okay."

"Is it alright if your dad is in the room?"

I nod. "I want him here."

"That's just fine. I want him here, too." He turned his head a little. "Why did you end up in the hospital?"

"I got burns," I said. I showed him my bandaged arms.

"That sounds really awful. Can you tell me how it happened?"

I looked at my father. "Answer honestly, Rosie. He's just trying to help."

No. He was just trying to rip our family apart.

"I helped put out a prairie fire."

"You must be very brave. What happened, though? At the fire?"

"My shoe came untied. I tripped." He scribbled onto the pad. I glared at his little pen tip wiggling in the air. "My father pulled me out of the fire."

Block. Move. Counter move. The pen tip stopped moving on the page. I'd taken a key piece from him.

"Your father pulled you out?"

"Uh-huh," I said. In truth, I didn't really know who pulled me out. I knew he drove me directly to the hospital, so I assumed it had been him. Either way, it obviously disrupted whatever narrative Sheriff Coulson created in his head.

"Mmm. How was your hospital stay?"

I didn't understand his move. I answered with as little information as possible.

"Good."

"What was it like?"

"Lot of white. White walls, bright lights, white coats."

"Did your father stay with you?"

"Yep."

"The whole time?"

Check. His rook in line with my king.

"Papa slept in a chair in my room," I said.

King moved. Rook takes my pawn.

"And did he sleep there every night?"

"Why does that matter?"

"Just making conversation."

"I don't like this conversation," I said, a little louder than I meant to.

"Rosie, it's alright," Papa tried. I ignored him.

"Why don't you just go back to town. We were just fine before you showed up."

My bishop. His queen in line. No chance to escape.

"How about just one more question, and then I'll be happy to go." I grinned triumphantly. This stupid man, with his stupid tan uniform, saddling up and leaving us alone. Only another minute. Maybe less.

"Just one?"

"Just one." Sheriff Coulson didn't have glasses, but I imagine him even now removing a pair of round spectacles and cleaning them on an untucked shirt tail. "Does your dad drink too much? I mean, does he drink too much around you?"

Knight takes bishop. Checkmate. I lost.

My father's voice quivered with rage. "You get the hell out of here and you don't come back, you rotten son of a bitch."

It didn't matter. Coulson had seen the expression on my face. Momentary, true, but the flash of pain and struggle would have been undeniable. He knew in that moment what I would take years to accept: my house was no home for a child.

The sheriff stood. "It appears I've crossed a line. I'll be going."

He stepped out the front door so quickly that my father could barely register it. Once the door shut, Paul's brain completed a reboot. He chased after the man, shouting insults and slurs as the car peeled out of the driveway.

Sheriff Coulson's behavior seemed strange then, and in light of learning about due process, it seems strange now. His visit, his conversation, his overly prying questions. They weren't the actions a cop would, or maybe even should, take. But he was not just some average cop. Sure, some asshole down at Social Services had done a check at our ranch a while back, but that didn't mean anything to him. He probably knew exactly what kind of man had driven to our ranch so long ago, the kind who doesn't even get out of his car for a wellness check.

No, that wouldn't sit well with our sheriff. Sheriff Coulson had the sand of an old lawman, the type you saw in our cowboy movies or in the Louis L'Amore novels I had just started to read. He was every bit the match to Paul Bauer, a real gunslinger in a world that doesn't seem to have them anymore. He was, at heart, an honest cowboy, the type who didn't so much care for laws as what was right, and he needed to look my father in the eye to understand the growing stack of reports and phone calls he was getting about Paul Bauer. Now he knew who my father was. All that remained was getting the law to fall in line with the truth.

23

THAT WAS THE END OF our day. My father wouldn't stop repeating the same phrases, peppered with the type of vulgar language that gets people canceled on Twitter. All of it revolved around his drinking and the fact that it was no cop's business if he had a beer or two after a hard day's work. Helen and Corey stayed for four or five of his rants, perhaps hoping in vain that he might wear himself out on the subject of that 'goddamned fucking puke'. Instead of slowing down, each repetition seemed to wind him up more. When he kicked one of the chairs across the room, Helen made a polite excuse about opening the restaurant and ushered Corey out the front door. Corey barely had time to look at me before her one hand shoved him through the same front door that Coulson had fled through less than an hour prior.

Paul opened a bottle almost immediately after they left.

***

THE NEXT MORNING I woke him. He slept on his chair, a plate of half-eaten oven-baked pizza sliding from his naked stomach.

"Looks like I stayed up a little late," Papa said. He pressed a hand to his forehead. "Want to hunt up some breakfast?" he asked.

"I want to go to school," I said.

Papa looked at me through one open eye. He set the plate on the floor beside him, stood up, stumbled into our bathroom. I could hear the sound of him pissing through the open door. Once he had finished, the toilet flushed. He walked out of the bathroom, into his bedroom, and shut the door.

***

I PUT TOGETHER the registration paperwork with the help of Opie. The librarian seemed distracted during the process. She smiled more than usual. After a little cajoling, I got her to focus on the task ahead. When I left the library, all Papa had to do was sign a couple of lines.

He signed the papers from a stool at the bar across the street. He bought us chili dogs, and we laughed at the bad cowboy music from Garth Brooks, someone Papa thought was even worse than a 'Sucker.' He was a 'Poser'. To him, that meant he had more money than a cowboy should. Either way, the jokes made our guts hurt and the day passed in bliss.

The actual transition to school wouldn't happen for another two weeks. I remember checking my first-day outfit at least twice a day, always changing one or two pieces of clothing. I had rotated my entire wardrobe at least once.

At first, they tried to put me in kindergarten. I politely explained that I already knew all of that. I had to take a set of tests in a small room next to the principal's office. After that, the school tried to put me in the fifth grade. I told the principal that if I wasn't in Corey's class, I wouldn't show up to school. He made a big deal about authority and talking back, but the fact of the matter was that I was just too goddamn stubborn. If I had gone through all the trouble of going to school, I was going to go with my friend. When he called my father about it, I heard a loud voice on the other end of the line say,

"Well, put her in the damned third grade then!" A dial tone rang out. By the second half of my first day, I was walking toward the room where Corey learned.

My walk into that classroom could be likened to the first step a character takes into a magical world. Like Bilbo Baggins, I was joining an adventure that promised to change me forever. The paper decorations on the wall, the cutout handprints of individual students with Crayola names identifying their maker, the rows of wooden desks facing a shining whiteboard, I expect that when I get to heaven, my room will look something very close to the way that classroom did. Here was community. Lines of children, all my age, turned to face me. Despite the nervous pit in my stomach, the tremble, the knowledge that I actually should have gone with a different shirt for my first day, I looked at every face and saw a potential friend. There, off to one side, sat Corey. His backpack sat on the chair next to him. The teacher waved at me.

"Hello. You must be Corey's friend. He insisted on saving you a seat," she said.

Oh the joy of those words. I had a friend. He waited for me.

"Why don't you get your stuff put in an open cubby and we'll let you introduce yourself in a minute."

The teacher, Miss Ernst, had the type of smile that said 'Come stay awhile. You're welcome here.' She moved up a year with Corey's class, which I thought was just splendid. The class introduced themselves a second time, and she explained that the day was mostly games to get to know one another. Since I was new, I would get to follow Corey and meet kids that way. We rotated around the room in shifts. One game was hopscotch spelling your name as you went through. Another was building a Lego house with three other people. All of them meant that by the end I knew a fair amount of names. A bell dismissed us for a final recess.

"I'm really glad you came to school," Corey said from the swing next to mine. His voice grew louder and softer as he moved back and forth.

24

THE NEXT MONTHS WERE THE happiest of my life, and also the most difficult. I wore long-sleeve shirts with gloves, and after a while the other kids stopped asking me why. My scars were covered, and with time the world already seemed to keep turning. It's strange how so many good things can mingle with so many bad. School meant new friends. I loved them all in a transient way. They had not been permanent in my life leading up to that moment, and a bit of me knew that all of them wouldn't hold a permanent place in my heart the way Corey or my father did. These people lived with me for a brief period. The times we read together, the recesses spent climbing monkey bars, these would always be solid moments, not threads weaving through the tapestry of my life.

Even moments can change things. This was also the time that everything grew darker. Papa pulled me out of school for every sale he could. I rode with him, his mood sour and unpredictable. One moment he and I would sing along to a song, then I would mention that a kid from class also liked Bob Segar, and the radio would go silent, and he would go silent too. He pouted. He stuck out his bottom lip and didn't respond when you asked him what was wrong. At a time in my life when I met more children my age, the biggest one I dealt with was my father.

The sales themselves weren't the same, either. Prices seemed to be on the rise. We spent more money on less machinery. It was one of those markets that made life difficult for jockeys like my father. Machinery seemed to be going directly to the producer, leaving middlemen like him scrambling. He wrung what money he could from tractors and sickle mowers, but with money tight, the sales grew more competitive. Gone were the days of roadside cafes and soda in the truck. Now we ate bologna sandwiches and packed plastic water bottles.

Paradoxically, at precisely the time when belts and money grew tighter, my father became more liberal with his bar room budget. He initially took me in with him. Eventually even he couldn't ignore the sideways glances, the mutterings. The simple fact is that a bar is no place for a little girl, and people knew, and in these small towns, people talked about it. One day, in a bar we had been in twice before, the bouncer turned us away. He wouldn't let me in.

This mercy proved a great harm. Papa never tried to take me into a bar again. That didn't mean he stopped going.

The next sale, a consignment auction on the north edge of Sioux Falls, started at 9:00 AM. Papa took us into town the day before. He unhitched his trailer in a hotel parking lot, and we drove to a hardware store. The sun was still in the west when we got there.

"Rosie, I am going to send you in to buy a lock for the trailer hitch and a couple of sockets," Papa said. He wrote down the sizes he wanted. Then he looked right in my eyes. "I'm heading out, so you're going to have to sit for a while. Do you have a book?"

I did, but I also had a deep desire not to sit in a store in the middle of the city at 4:00pm. I tried to protest. He spoke before I could even get a word out.

"I need you to be a big girl and get the job done."

That meant that it wasn't an option. I could beg, plead, cry, stomp my feet. It wouldn't matter. Complaining would only prolong the inevitable. I got out of the truck. In protest, I slammed my door. The piece of paper was clutched in one hand, a fifty-dollar bill and The Adventures of Huckleberry Finn were in the other. I marched inside.

The job itself took less than ten minutes. The longest part was learning why the black sockets cost so much more money than the silver ones. After a bald employee helped me, I went to the front.

A black woman with a bright smile sat behind the counter. She looked older than Grandma Helen. Gray hair covered her scalp. As I rang up the items, she glanced over her glasses at me.

"You doing a project, Missy?" No one had ever called me Missy before.

"No, ma'am," I said.

"Ma'am. Ain't you sweet." She grabbed a Milky Way candy bar from the display and tossed it in the bag without ringing it up. I looked at the snow outside and my own winter clothes.

"Can I sit here and read while I wait for my dad?" I asked. She nodded at me.

The sounds of the store are the most visceral part of the memory for me. A mop bucket rolled across a linoleum floor. The periodic, unrhythmic opening and closing of automatic doors. Each time brought a wave of cold air through me. Even the ding of a cash drawer opening is stuck in my mind today. I sat staring at words that wouldn't sit still on the page. My mind wandered to whatever place he took at whatever dump that called itself a saloon. I wondered if he leered at a waitress. I wondered if he thought that just one more drink would actually mean one more.

An hour passed. Two. The sun set. Darkness filled the outside of the store. The streetlights reflected yellow in the drifted snow. Only the pile out front of the doors glowed red, a gift of the enormous neon sign nailed to the face of the building. I did not weep. There were no more tears left for life. I had passed beyond grief. Only acceptance, and a little ache in my heart, remained. The night grew long. Had it been three hours? It had been long enough that the cashier looked at me more frequently. Soon she would pick up the phone and dial a number, and someone in a uniform would show up. I could sit there and wait for that. My mind traveled back to Missouri, to a look in a bartender's eyes when he said the words 'foster care'.

That was no place for me.

I stood up, put my book in the plastic bag that held the sockets and the hitch lock. If Papa was really concerned, we should have gone straight back to the hotel to lock up our trailer. He gave me this job so I would have something to do.

At the time, my father had an old flip phone. I went to the counter.

"May I call my father, please?" I asked. The woman nodded. She pressed a key on the phone. When she asked for his number, I gave it to her. She typed it in and handed me the phone.

"Hello?" his voice said. The sounds of chattering people made it hard to hear him.

"Come pick me up," I said.

"Rosie, I'll be there in a bit," he said.

"Now," I said. "They're going to close soon." I had no idea if this was true. I knew that if he didn't, I planned to walk back to the hotel, freezing air be damned.

"Rosie..." he tried again.

"Right now. How far is the drive?"

"I'm ten minutes away," he said.

"You've got fifteen to get here," I said. I handed the phone back to the cashier. "Thank you." She gave me a funny look, then hung up the phone. I went back to my spot on a red bench inside the door. When I opened the book, I actually read a chapter.

***

PAPA SHOWED UP buzzed but not drunk. I walked outside so that the store workers wouldn't see him. He tried to light into me when I climbed in.

"Listen here, girl. I'm your father. I should get some respect for..."

"If you hadn't come to get me, I know the cashier was going to call the police," I interrupted. "Is that what you want?"

He fell silent. There's no way either of us could know if she actually would have called the cops or if it was simply a gut feeling. We both knew, though, that if she did, it would mean a separation. Neither would argue otherwise. The only conversation we had that night was about which movie to watch on the tiny hotel TV.

***

THAT SALE IS a moment where the balanced scales of my life, order and chaos, collapse. We drove to the field in the morning. Papa didn't use either the hitch lock or the sockets I had bought the night before, something that wasn't lost on me even at that age. We listened to a tape of Gospel Music sung by Elvis Presley.

"Why don't we go to church?" I asked him.

"Church?" he chuckled. "Buncha suckers there. Capital 'S' Suckers."

"Why?"

"Why?" Paul shook his head. "Why. Rosie, they stand around facing a preacher, some acne-ridden kid who's never seen the real world or an old man with one foot already in their great beyond, and they sing hymns, and they pass around a plate to take your money. Then, when they've collected money from the poor, they spend it on a house for the preacher. It's a scam."

It didn't sound anything like the way Corey had described it to me once. He said church was a place where sick people went to get better. When I asked him about my burns, he told me it was for 'spiritually sick people'. He had gotten a sad look in his eyes.

"I think my mother was sick like that," Corey said quietly. "Before the crash."

Looking at my father, I thought he fit in that category too. Yet I said nothing.

"Do you like these hymns?" I asked. We had listened to that gospel album for about a month.

"Sure. I like the music even if I don't like the imaginary friend they're about." He tapped the wheel. "Remember this, girl. If your head's in the clouds, your feet ain't on the ground."

The empty platitude didn't placate me. We pulled into the field.

The sale itself was unremarkable. We bought a tractor, but not a great one. The profit would pay for the trip and a little extra. What stuck out was paying.

Emma sat behind the counter, one of her rotating romance books in her hand. Despite the cold, she wore her coat partially unzipped. My father ran a hand through his hair before walking up to the stand.

"Hey, Emma," he said.

"Paul!" she said. She ran around and gave him a hug, which I thought was a very odd thing to do to a paying customer. "Samantha! How are you!"

"Hi, Emma," I said formally.

"EmEm, remember?" she said, wagging a finger at me. My stomach tightened. I clenched my jaw in a way that turned me into the image of my father. Emma never noticed. She only had eyes for Papa. "How's business?"

"Great," my father lied. "Machinery is moving, and I can't keep it on my ranch for long it seems. Soon as something sells, someone else is stopping by to buy it."

That was a partial truth. We couldn't keep machinery on our yard, but when someone stopped by after a piece was sold, it was almost always to offer less than we paid before asking for the number of the next buyer. Everyone was trying to undercut everyone.

Emma grinned. "Business has been alright for us." Her voice got lower so Lionel wouldn't hear. "They are making money hand over fist, but I think they won't keep me on long."

"Why?" Paul asked, matching her tone.

"I keep bringing up pay discrepancies. Lionel makes a shitpile, but it doesn't get spread around." She failed to mention that Lionel paid her more than a fair wage for her work, especially since she'd left work early at least twice a week for the past two months. She also didn't say that her pay tended to go directly into her nose most months. All of this I would learn from Lionel himself, years later, over a cup of coffee.

"You're probably just stuck too much in the city mindset," Paul said. "What you need is some fresh air and a timeout from a corporation."

"That sounds wonderful," Emma said. Paul wrote down his cell phone number and slid it over to her.

"Come see the ranch sometime. It would be good for you."

She did drive out to the ranch. It wasn't a visit, though. When her car, a nearly new Cadillac with bright chrome rims, pulled into our driveway, it didn't leave for nearly a year. Emma moved into my house a week after the sale, and the ticking clock of my father's life began to count down.

25

HERE IS A LAST FAREWELL to a chance at good things. If our life is the herd, then Emma is the sweeping blizzard. Sure some of the cows had keeled over already, but her entry into the daily routine of our lives is the moment when things don't fall apart but rather collapse. She is the acceleration, the brick on the gas pedal, the lead up to the last standoff and the goddamn gun and the held hand. She is the final bad influence. She approaches my song, and the words get darker, and the death gets nearer, and I can hear every note in a minor key haunting me with the approach of the grand finale.

I went to school the day Emma pulled into our driveway. I didn't even know she had driven out to the middle of the state. At the end of the day, my class walked out the front door. Our little bodies lined the sidewalk. Pickup truck after pickup truck drove by. Kids disappeared one by one.

I didn't notice Ophelia until she was next to me. She wore a puffy green overcoat. Mushroom earrings dangled beneath a yellow stocking cap. I grinned when I saw her.

"Opie!" I shouted. She got down on a knee to give me a hug. "Why are you here?"

"I came to see you," she said, laughing. "Hello, Corey."

"Hi," Corey said. His cheeks turned red. More red. They were already flushed from the Dakota cold.

"I heard," Ophelia said. "That you went to a sale the other day."

"Who told you that?" I asked.

"Your teacher. I tried to bring you something then. I've been hoping to get down here since." She held out a small package wrapped in red paper. "Consider it a late Christmas present. Or an early Christmas present for next year."

The group of kids dwindled. There was no sign of Grandma Helen's beater car or my father's truck.

"You can open it," Ophelia encouraged. I pulled at the wrapping with my pink mittens. It tore with a satisfying sound. Inside was a tiny flip phone, the type that you could pre-load minutes on with green gift cards sold at gas station counters.

"Thanks," I said, a little taken aback. I had never wanted a phone nor thought I needed one. Who would I call?

"I put my telephone number in there," Ophelia said as if she could read my mind. "I've been...seeing someone...and he thought that you might need something like this."

"Thank you," I said. My tone was more grateful the second time.

"You can call me anytime. And if you need more minutes, let me know and I will have some by the library." Ophelia squeezed my hand.

She had tears in her eyes that day. I realized that there were not a whole lot of reasons to move to a place like Lemmon. People didn't come to town. They left town. Some part of me had already accepted that my story would be a leaving story too. Not hers, though. Before me was a woman who had no family here, no history here, who had materialized in my life as a librarian with no background.

She came from somewhere bad.

I didn't know anything else from the way she squeezed my hand. I just knew that the grip, so desperate, so desiring to be a reassurance even though we both understood that neither of us could change reality, I knew that was the grip of someone with whom I had some kinship. In this gesture, we became sisters. Ophelia's life grieved me, and mine grieved her, more than words could have expressed on that little public sidewalk. She was trying to say 'I love you. I wish life loved you. I wish life gave you strawberries and kindness.' And when I hugged her hand close, I tried to say 'It's no one's fault, the smashing glass, the cracking flesh in cool November winds, the stench of bile mixed with sweat, all of that was nobody's fault, especially not yours.'

"Well," she said roughly. "I don't see your grown-ups. Corey, can I drive you and Sam home?"

"Grandma's probably busy at the restaurant. Can you call and let her know I'm on the way?" Corey asked. Ophelia pulled out her own cell phone. It was painted like a ladybug. She dialed the number Corey gave her. After a brief, loud conversation, she shut the phone.

"She said that she's got customers coming out of her ears. You want a ride?" Corey nodded. "What about you, Rosie? Do you want me to call your father?"

"We can just go," I said. He wasn't on time. That meant he wasn't on the way. My father spent his life oscillating between the promptness of a boy scout to forgetting me completely. Now that it was just the three of us and Miss Ernst on the sidewalk, I felt comfortable assuming today meant the latter.

Ophelia drove a purple Toyota Forerunner. One bumper sticker said 'Where the HECK is Wall Drug'. The other advertised a minor politician in Rhode Island. Corey sat in the back seat. I climbed into the passenger seat. We all buckled out seatbelts. Ophelia selected a CD from a black leather case and put it in the slot. It was the type of CD with sharpie marker on the front. Someone had burned her an album, or maybe she had made it herself. She pushed a button on the dash, and my seat grew warm. I had never seen heated seats before.

Of all the things to come from the radio speakers, I did not expect Metallica. The power chord of 'Master of Puppets' filled the cabin.

"What the hell?" Corey said from the back seat.

"Hey, no need for that language," Ophelia said. Then, a little sheepishly, she looked at me. "I like Rock and Roll."

"Awesome!" I said. I reached over and turned the volume up. Corey laughed.

"You're both nuts," he said.

"I can't hear you," I called back. I did a wicked air guitar solo. Corey laughed harder. He clutched his gut. Ophelia removed her hat and bobbed her head to the music. Her hair, always kept in a tight ponytail or bun, went wild. When the chorus hit, we both sang along. Corey clapped off the rhythm, and we were happy for the accompaniment.

AC/DC, Foo Fighters, and Iron Maiden sang us down the icy roads. This was a happy note in our songs. We howled like wild animals. The beat and the strumming electrified the car. We felt alive. We felt together. No one wanted the trip to end. In our own way, each of us fantasized about the car continuing down the road, taking us beyond the broken down restaurant, beyond the gravel turn off, maybe even up into the sky like the movie 'Grease'. We wanted the wheels to bring us to a new world, one where lights didn't come in neon, where the bright morning would crash over a soft countryside, and all of us would be a family in action rather than in the simple lines of family names on birth certificates. We wanted no motorcycle crashes taking mothers away from their baby boys. We wanted Grandmas with both hands. We wanted fathers with their sideways humor and no booze in the whole damn house. We wanted a chance for our family to take back the terrible days, the dark evenings. We wanted loneliness to be banished from our lives and our thoughts and our kitchens. Oh God, if wanting were enough, then we wanted more than any people ever did. The desire in our hearts brought us close to one another. This drive down an American highway was communion with the world God made in the first place, the one people could have had.

It ended. We needed to turn into the restaurant. We needed to leave Corey at the front door, his green glove raised in sad farewell. We needed to turn down the gravel road, Ophelia and I contemplating the wiry branches of trees or the snow collected along the barbed wire.

"Opie?" I asked. We were about five minutes from the house.

"What's up?"

"The man you're seeing. Is it Sheriff Coulson?"

Ophelia chewed her lower lip. She was deciding whether or not she should lie.

"Yes," she said, landing on the truth.

"Do you love him?"

"I don't know if..." She giggled, but not in the fake way Emma did when my father spoke to her. It sounded happy, without strings attached. "Yes. I think I do. We've only dated a couple of months, and I think I love him." She shook her head. "You must think I'm rather silly."

"I don't think love is ever silly," I said. "I think loving someone is the most serious thing you can do."

Strangely, I didn't hate her or Sheriff Coulson. I had hated him when he came by to ask about my scars. Hate is strange at that age. It doesn't take off its coat or hat in your home, and it leaves as if it has somewhere very important to be. At that time, I was happy because Ophelia was happy.

"You're very smart for your age, you know that?"

"I don't feel my age." I picked at my mitten. Beneath, my hand had an appearance somewhat like raw hamburger. "I feel older."

"You're not alone," Ophelia said. "I'm sorry that it feels that way. But you aren't."

"Course I'm not," I said. "I've got you."

26

EMMA'S CAR HAD BEEN PARKED next to my father's truck. I recognized it from the auctions we'd been to. I didn't say anything about it to Ophelia. Before I got out of the car, I squeezed her hand one more time.

"You know you can call me anytime," she said. I nodded. "Okay. I'll see you later?"

"I'll be in this week. I only have two chapters left in Huck Finn." I hopped out of the vehicle. Cold air fought and won against the warmth of Ophelia's car. Briefly, I wondered when the cold would leave, honoring a generation-spanning Midwest tradition of complaining about the weather. I waved from the front porch. Ophelia's car waited until after I went inside.

Noises came from the direction of my father's room. I called out loudly.

"Papa!" The noise stopped. Whispered voices came through.

"Is that Sammy?"

"The doors are thin," my father's voice responded. The rest of the conversation was too quiet to hear.

The living room was a disaster. When I left, it hadn't been that great, I'll admit, but it was nothing like this. Three suitcases lay open on the floor. They held clothes from brands I had never heard of. All looked expensive. A record rotated on a turntable. The needle sat at the middle. It bounced a little.

Scratching echoed through the speakers. Dense air made my coat feel too heavy. Someone had left the furnace cranked high. The overflowing trash, one of the few chores Papa was supposed to handle that I refused to do anymore, stank. He had promised me it would be out two days ago. Bad broccoli smell, sweat, heat, the whole house had become a hell. I had no idea that the following weeks would only see it deteriorate from there.

Papa's door creaked open. Through the crack, I saw Emma hurrying to put a bra on. My father stepped out. He pulled the door shut behind him with a click. He stood motionless in the hallway for a moment. The top three buttons of his shirt were undone. Barefoot, he walked to the living room.

"Back from school?" he asked. I nodded. He lit a cigarette. His eyes had the glassy look that only comes after half the bottle these days. The man got his money's worth out of his liver. Tolerance only meant that he consumed more now. Tobacco smell mixed unpleasantly with the garbage. Together, it wasn't the same safe smell. It was safety gone rotten. Sweat covered his semi-exposed chest. He seemed frustrated more than embarrassed. "Who brought you here?"

"Ophelia," I said.

"Could have called first."

"Could have." I swallowed the lump in my throat. She shouldn't have had to call. You should have picked me up. I thought. You damned selfish bastard. Of the many lessons he taught me, none were so thorough as the use of a cuss word. My whole life had trained me in their proper placement.

"You should go..." he struggled to get a bottle from the counter. His fumbling fingers annoyed me. I pushed the bottle closer to make this end faster. "You want to play outside?"

"It's winter," I said curtly.

"Hmm," Paul said. He took a long drink. The door opened. Emma walked out. Her hair was a mess and her shirt was on both backwards and inside out. I stared at her. She seemed unable to meet my eye, though not from shame. Her eyes bounced around the room, never settling on anything for more than a brief moment. When I moved to New York years later, someone would use the word 'tweaking' to describe a homeless man outside of a convenience store a few blocks from my dorm room. The man looked like Emma did now, as if she expected the walls to turn into cockroaches at any moment and so she best be prepared to bolt for an exit if necessary.

"Hi," I said.

"Hi, Sammy. Ham Sammy," she said, then laughed at her own joke. I looked from her to my father. Whatever new problem this presented, I had neither the patience nor the ability to deal with it.

"I'll be in the shop," I said. I wandered outside. The sun would be down in a short while. The outside cold felt worse than it had when I left Opie's car. I don't know why, but the house's heat must have been set at eighty degrees. The bitter wind bit my exposed face. I stomped through the snow to our shop.

A cow mooed from the barn. I changed direction and trudged towards the cattle. Ice covered the water trough. A group of heifers pushed each other around. No doubt they were thirsty. I grabbed the steel T-Post my father should have used to break the ice. It took time to chip away at it. I wanted to cry. If I didn't get the job done, the cows would die. Where the world had felt so light earlier, it seemed all the heavier as it resettled onto my tiny shoulders. I kept my tears inside and got the work done. I laid the post back in the corner. The cows stuck their heads through the gates and took long, slurping gulps of the dirty water. They would live. I had bought them another day. I left for the shop.

Papa hadn't even shoveled the snow from in front of the door. I grabbed a plastic snow shovel and began to tunnel into the building. It took enough time that my hands felt numb in my mittens. Damp cloth was in the process of refreezing around my ankles.

I made it inside. Darkness filled every corner of the shop. My hands fumbled for the light switch. My heart thumped in my chest. An overactive imagination told me of rattlesnakes who never burrowed waiting by the door, of boney coyotes foaming at the mouth, holding in their howls until the first bite of a little girl. The fluorescents buzzed to dim life, and I let out my breath. Even inside, it came out a puff of mist. My hands shook. It wasn't the kind shake of a chilly afternoon, or being nervous, or excited. It was the violent tremble that a doctor would have recognized as a precursor to hypothermia. The other symptoms showed up soon after. I knew I needed to start my father's propane heater. Everything felt foggy in my head as if I had just woken up.

The air felt like walking through syrup. My hands became worse. The numbness in them became pin-prick pain when I tried to open the nozzle on the propane tank. I thought I had only been outside for ten minutes. It must have been longer. I couldn't think. Everything felt too foggy. Too foggy. I wanted to lie down to sleep.

A smart person would have tried to get back to the house. I didn't. Some part of me might have realized the danger I was in, but it didn't seem to fully compute. My thumb depressed the red igniter switch. It clicked. Some nights I wake up screaming from a nightmare, and no matter what I dream, the bad dreams are always accompanied by the repeated clicking of an electric igniter. I pressed again. No flame. The smell of propane made my eyes open a little, but not enough. Just a little nap couldn't hurt.

I pressed the button again. The heater flared to life with a sound like a jet engine. My teeth chattered so terribly that they hurt.

At that moment, it wouldn't be an exaggeration to say that the local library saved my life. I remembered a book where a character fell into a frozen lake. He had to get naked after so that he could warm up. I removed my wet boots, wet snow pants, and wet socks. My jeans were only slightly damp at the ankles. I pulled an office chair as close to the heater as I dared. Next, I pulled off my mittens. I couldn't tell if the skin was that pink because of my scars or the weather. My hands itched. Doctor Olson said they may itch at times. He also said not to scratch at it, no easy feat.

The shop creaked in the wind. It made a kind of prairie song all its own. Every place has a song, and the song of my old home is forever the groan of corrugated steel at war with nature herself, a propane jet fighting the law of entropy, the gentle sobs of a little girl who had already given too many tears to the world and could only spare these tiny cries. The light grew brighter and I grew warmer. For an hour, I sat listening to the wind battle the building. Inside was a little heat, a little girl, a shelter against everything outside the four walls. In the shop, life might have still been the way it was years before. A film of dust covered the tractors and the tools, sure, but they still sat in the same place.

Looking there, writing of yet another near-death to the elements, I begin to see my young life as a long chain of weeping events. Childhood for me is tears, and tears are not anything more than acceptance of the facts. They are an acknowledgment that no matter how much you love a lie, it can't change the truth. I blame Emma for those months, but the untended shop is the truth, and I told you I would tell it.

My father's spiral began before she moved into my home and my life. I could see it in the dust, in the unsold machinery, in all the work left undone. It was in the trailer with a tractor still on it. It was in the eternally growing pile of plastic whiskey bottles by the door or next to the workbench or on the table. Paul Bauer already rolled down the hill. Emma just cut the brake lines. Like so many nights before, I laid my head in my ugly hands, and I wept.

27

THE NEXT MONTHS SAW SUCH a rapid decline, I can barely pinpoint what steps took us to the sale. I know how it was the day Emma moved in. Chores not done, cattle not fed, and machinery not sold. I also know what the living room looked like when we left for the sale.

Everything was worse.

The first time I saw the white lines, I thought they were sugar. My father preferred downers to uppers, so usually it would be Emma with a bloody nose in the bathroom when I got up to brush my teeth. She insisted I call her 'EmEm'. I would have preferred to call her 'bitch', but what good would it do?

Dirty clothes lay across most open surfaces. Our diet, never great in the first place, transformed into exclusively microwave meals. I tried to keep a clean home at first. I would pick up clothes and place them in a basket. One of them would knock the basket to the ground on their way to the kitchen for a midnight snack, refusing even the simple courtesy of fixing their own mistake. When the sink grew too full of dishes, we bought a bulk pack of Styrofoam plates and plastic silverware. The cold weather kept them inside most of the days.

Usually, Papa picked me up from school, but four times in that month Emma came to town in her Cadillac. On those days, she would grab me, then drive me to the opposite end of town where a dollar store sat. Parking right next to a shitty red car, she would pull an envelope from her purse, wink at me, and say 'Our secret' before counting out twenties for the man who waited for her. He passed her a bag, and we would drive exactly the speed limit the whole way to the ranch.

We only went to Grandma Helen's restaurant once after Emma arrived. Helen might have been a scary-looking woman, but she wasn't stupid. She knew what Paul and Emma got up to at all hours of the day, and she knew what that meant for her. I could have caught a chill from her attitude when she slammed the plates down in front of us.

School seemed the only escape. I couldn't believe my ears when one of my classmates complained about being there. I wanted to grab him by the shoulders, to shake him and scream Don't you know how lucky you are? Don't you know how awful it can get out there?

One morning, still a little buzzed from the night before, Papa shook me awake.

"Hey, Lemondrop," he said, and I hoped for a second that the details had been a nightmare, that the acceleration of our days towards the tree of reality was nothing more than a bad dream. I woke into the nightmare, though, and there was no denying the sound of the woman's hoarse voice singing Britney Spears in our shower. "We've got a sale today."

"Am I going to school?" I pulled on my gloves.

"Nah," Papa said. "You'll ride with us."

"I want to go to school," I said. He either didn't hear me or pretended not to. Papa opened my closet and pushed my t-shirts around.

"Get dressed quick," he said.

"I want to go to school," I repeated.

"Hurry up, girl. I'm not going to tell you again." Papa left the room.

That was one of the greatest tragedies of my childhood, of any childhood for that matter. I was young. When I spoke, a grown up didn't think it was necessary to listen.

We left the ranch behind. Paul and Emma's bodies smashed into mine. Claustrophobia would be too intense to describe the feeling, but it was something close to it. I looked back on my house and saw it with eyes that weren't mine. That morning it didn't look like home. I pulled every memory I could from the image, dulled the colors of laughter until all that remained was a picture of how it must look to someone driving through our yard for the first time. The house leaned to the left. The shingles needed repairs years ago. The paint fell in chunks from the siding. The whole thing was surrounded by dirty snow and trees that held no leaves. To watch a childhood home become a place like any other is a horror, and I turned away from it.

We didn't listen to music. Papa and Emma looked over at each other every half hour or so and snickered. Once at school two kids told a joke to each other that made no sense to me. When I asked about it, they said 'You wouldn't get it, you weren't there.' That felt the same way. The road disappeared behind us or appeared before us, depending on how you wanted to look at it. No one said a word until we crossed the Missouri, and then it was only Emma saying she had to 'tinkle'. Papa pulled off at a gas station and she trotted inside. When she got to the door, she turned back and waved at my father.

"I don't like her," I said suddenly. He turned to me.

"What?"

"I don't like her."

"That's not nice," my father said. I debated if I wanted a fight. The part of me that did was too tired, too worn out. I dropped the subject. Papa lit a cigarette. Childhood could be measured in uncountable cigarettes between his lean fingers.

"Give me one of those," I said. He looked at me.

"You keep away from these."

"You don't."

"They aren't good for you."

Maybe I was wrong. Maybe the fight in me wasn't too tired yet. "Are they good for you?"

"I shouldn't smoke them."

"You do, though."

"I know I smoke, Rosie." He pinched his nose. The cigarette got close to but did not burn his forehead.

"Smoking kills people. We had an officer tell us about it in school one day."

"You need a cop to tell you that?" He retorted.

"I think you should quit smoking," I said.

"I should quit smoking."

"Why don't you?"

"Jesus Christ, girl, what's got into you?" he snapped.

"Do you think that if you smoke, you won't get lung cancer like everyone else? Or heart disease? Or throat cancer?"

"Samantha, drop it," he said. I was on a roll though. Every gross plate of half-eaten supper that my sock found in the mornings, the trips to the dollar store with 'EmEm-almost-like-the-candy', the fucking dishes, they fueled the bonfire of my voice. I inherited many things from my father. I got his eyes, his love of music, his poor dance moves after a couple of drinks. And his white-hot rage.

"Do you think you're special?" I was close to shouting. "Do you think that she isn't bad news because it's you? That you can just drink all day and it won't change anything? The cows won't die? The chores will magically do themselves?"

It was a flinch. Nothing more. His right hand moved towards the wheel. My father didn't hit me, but we both saw the backhand that could have been. I got my anger from him, and I saw it reflected in the eyes we shared. Two Bauers sat in a truck. A father so close to hitting his daughter and breaking the last trust they both had for one another. He would become the eternal bad father, and I the eternal victim daughter. We would be for one another an accusation and nothing more. Was this the same two people who drove the hills of Missouri? Did these two dance a jig to vinyl records in a living room? Did they love each other still?

Of course, they loved each other. Of course, I loved him. I saw the hand, the pain on his face like a flash of lightning, bright and visceral and brief.

"I don't want you to die," I said. It sounded so basic, so childish. But for all my childhood pretending at being grown-up, all I could be was the age I was.

I was angry. I was afraid, and I didn't know how to say it.

"Emma's coming back," he said. She climbed into the cab with a loud 'whoo!'. Her eyes bounced around. She checked her reflection in the mirror and wiped a small speck of white from her nostril.

We didn't talk the rest of the way to Aberdeen.

***

THAT SALE WOULD be the last time I saw Lionel for many years. The next time I saw him, I would walk with a cane, the aluminum kind that has four rubber feet. Those tiny four helped balance the one of mine that had a quarter size hole through it. When we ate our pancakes, we both thought back to the sale. The auction was two months before the pistol, before Corey, before my father and Emma and the sheriff like some god-damned movie.

Each of us could only wonder at what might have been.

There is no 'might have been', though. The world doesn't work that way. It deals in absolute reality. The sale had an opportunity for a different path, but no one took it, and we stayed along our trajectory toward the fall.

Papa found a spot at the back of a line of pickups. The sale was in full swing. We didn't even make it to sales on time anymore. The crowd contained all the usual suspects. Local farmers came dressed in T-shirts. Dirt loved these men. It clung to their boots, their hands, their mustaches. The machinery all looked the same. They sold two nice tractors right away, the type that went for the price of a house. Papa watched but never bid. Emma stayed in the truck.

We didn't get coffee or hot chocolate. None of the people had changed, but we had. Papa didn't make a point to talk to the man down the line. Each of these people were no longer our neighbors. They were our competition. Every item someone else bid on tightened his frown. The sale didn't hold the bounce of fun but rather the tense struggle of a wrestling match.

Lionel, up in the auctioneer's truck, called out his familiar chant. Papa took a drink from a flask, then raised it for another bid. Lionel pointed at him.

"We've got thirty, gotta be thirty-five hundred, thirty-five hundred, thirty-five, thirty-five hundred, would-ya-give thirty-five anywhere now, thirty-five dollar-bid-now thirty-five." Snow crunched beneath my boots, half sludge from the trampling of fifty pairs of feet. I adjusted my hat. Papa bought a tractor.

They used one of their common ringmen for a cashier. He typed Papa's name in and we waited. When the invoice printed, he didn't clap. He just took our check.

Lionel walked over to us. "Hey, Paul. Whaddya know?"

"Hey, Richy," my father said. We walked towards the orange tractor that my father now owned.

"I saw you had a stowaway today."

"Hmm," my father said. Lionel adjusted his cowboy hat. When the sun broke through the clouds, his silver bolo tie flashed an irregular pattern.

"Paul, I think we should talk about her," he said. He looked like a man testing the ice across a river. Each step might be the wrong one. The wrong one meant plunging into death. "She worked for me for a long time."

"Seems to be doing just fine for herself," Papa said coolly.

"She's bad news," Lionel blurted. "I don't mean to overstep, Paul, but she did a lot of..." His eyes flashed to me. The man actually spelled the word, as if I didn't know what the letters meant. "She did a lot of D-R-U-Gs. It wasn't pretty. I don't think you want that around your girl."

"You do overstep," My father said. We had arrived at the tractor. He pulled himself up the steps. It cranked over but wouldn't start in the cold.

Lionel opened his mouth as if to say something. The world, the future, life itself hung in the balance. My father was a good buyer. He took home items other people wouldn't. He wasn't the kind of customer a business could afford to piss off. And he lived with a woman who was bad news, who did D-R-U-Gs, who skipped work for a little sugar that wasn't sugar, who no doubt had made passes at many more men than my father. Lionel had his choice. Lionel could speak now or like Pilate before Christ say nothing and damn himself in such a sin.

Lionel said nothing.

Oh God in heaven, so far from this little piece of Dakota earth, Lionel said nothing.

My father started the tractor, and we loaded it on the trailer. Within an hour, we were on the road towards the ranch.

28

THE STORY OF EMMA IS worse than I care to admit. I'm a coward. I don't want to drag you through the shrill laughter, the long months, money flowing like a river from our front door all the way into the pockets of men in parking lots or along field approaches. My father began to have his own bloody noses. Pop music blared through our ranch house, ugly autotuned shit that dared filled the space that once held Marty Robbins and Waylon Jennings. It couldn't fill those boots, by my estimate.

The music and the not-quite-sugar brought men and women into our home. I would wake some mornings and find them draped on top of the ever-present laundry. They had too much or too little weight, too few teeth, tattoos along their arms. All of them were young. All of them had no jobs or shit jobs. I recognized the cashier from the convenience store lying on our coffee table one bright Tuesday. He didn't wear any clothes save for a pair of once-white underwear that didn't cover him well. His pimply face twitched when I walked passed.

I began to move through the house like a ghost. Every step became a dance. I avoided the parts of the floor that creaked, the bottles that grew in piles in one corner, the men. I didn't like the looks in their eyes, as if their souls had already passed through the mortal world, leaving only shambling husks of people and grieving daughters behind.

One day a man who had a little too much of EmEm's powder came pounding on my door. His fist left a hole in the hollow core. He shouted things you can't write in books, that you shouldn't write in books. He was descriptive.

Papa chased him outside with his pistol before he could do more damage. That evening, we taped blue construction paper over the hole.

Then came the house party.

Emma picked me up from school late one afternoon. She drove her Cadillac passed the dollar store, passed the church, passed the library and the bar. We came to rest in front of a home with a leftward lean. Shingles like a ratty quilt draped themselves over the roof. A lonely swing set blew in the wind. Outside, the cold air pierced our clothes. Spring sometimes forgot to warm the air, and the evening could have been winter even though we had nearly finished out the month of March.

"Ham Sammy," EmEm said, tapping her fingers along the leather steering wheel. "Samantha. Sam. Since it's just us girls, I wanted to know if you can keep a secret."

"Um..." I said, not sure how to respond.

"Um makes you sound dumb," she chattered. Her life was made up of empty words. She was a chattering chicken, out of place and domestic in this wild land. She was all squawk, all noise. "I want to know if you can keep a secret. From other people."

"Like Helen?" I asked.

"Yeah, and also others. Like if anyone asks, you have to keep this to yourself. Even policemen." An image of a spider on a web, and all his small spider minions, flashed through my mind. I didn't want to leave my father even then. Some part of me still believed that the world hadn't ended, that he might come back to me, that we might sing together once more.

"I guess," I said. The words had barely left my mouth before she spoke.

"Great. Let's go party." She opened the door and got out. I didn't move. She poked her head back into the car. "C'mon girl. You need to loosen up."

The house seemed wrong. It was a bad part of the song. I could tell just by looking at it that love had left. Inside would be something else. My body tensed.

"I don't want to go in there."

"Sam, I hate to be 'that girl', but I am a grown-up. You need to listen. Let's go." Emma walked around the car and held my door open. What other choice was there? I left the Cadillac, and even though I hated that car, it felt like leaving safety.

The snow, still clinging to the earth, crunched beneath my feet. The door opened to a room of blasting music, all synth. Emma walked in like she owned the place. I trotted behind, forgotten almost as soon as the door closed behind me.

The room felt claustrophobic. People sat on coffee tables or made out in the middle of the room. Some sweaty shirtless man wailed when he lost at beer pong. Skunk smells permeated the walls. Over it all, dim yellow light cast every face in sickly shades. Dead people filled the room. They had tight skin. They had hungry eyes. They moved, and I wondered if they had one foot already in that great beyond. These were coyote men, all ribs and teeth, all tricks, and a part of me thought back to a spider story and wondered if a web or a pair of gaping jaws made much of a difference when one was being devoured.

Someone at a breakfast bar handed me a cup. It burned my throat. In that shanty disguised as a house, I had my first drink of whiskey. I also had my second drink, and third, and fourth.

You've been drunk, I'm sure. Or you will be drunk. Or you will live your whole life without tasting that forbidden water, and I will hate you for that because jealousy can make you hate. That night is my first drink. That night is my first real step into my father's world. I lived as these dogs lived, rabid, wild, bristling arm hair while the music blared. God, once I listened to country music about love, now the men in the music used words Papapaul always said

I should never use. They sang about fucking while the people in the living room moved their hips against one another.

Emma had disappeared into an upstairs room. Once I saw my father, an empty bottle of fireball dangling from his fingers, but to this day, I don't know if he recognized me through the liquor. He only stared ahead. Do I believe he saw anything that night? I don't know. Perhaps he saw a chance to play a trick. Perhaps he felt himself carried towards an awaiting fire as I did, but felt he still could escape, still could jump up at the last second before becoming steak. Or maybe he saw yellowing drywall, people smoking weed, and some poor fool's little girl in the middle of a house party.

I wandered the house, passing people in various states of drunkenness and debauchery. I recognized the bartender from Papapaul's favorite spot to drink in town. I recognized a janitor from the school. The music thumped through the house. It felt like a heartbeat gone irregular. It felt like a disease.

The music, the booze, the young kid with a strange-looking pipe, a stench like burning plastic. This place felt different than the shop that winter, but no less dangerous. Death could find me here, the same way it would surely find all these people. I could lay down, could rest, and let it sweep me away gently. My stomach ached.

And my head. The room spun. My feet felt paradoxically heavy and light. I thought about the agent who came to our farm before, the one from DSS. Could he overlook this? He had not returned for many years. He had no desire to do anything. None of these people did. They looked on, they bore witness through a shade of alcohol or drugs, and not a single one did a thing. There is damnation in that ugly phrase 'someone else will do something'.

I couldn't stay here. Hands brushed me in places I did not want. I saw the face of a man years ago, with tobacco juice falling down his lower lip, with a wide-brimmed hat and a beer gut, with a voice saying 'Do you like puppies, Sam? I got a real pretty dog back at my truck.' I saw a shaking waitress ask if 'that man' was my father before my first sale. I saw the hole in my door, I heard the things that man said that made my skin feel like a sin. This place held death.

I wanted to live. I wanted to leave.

"What's wrong?" A voice asked. The man it belonged to nearly scraped his head on the low ceiling. He reminded me of a buffalo, some rare thing, all brawn but no malice. He wore Adidas sweatpants, a shirt with Mount Rushmore on it, and a baseball cap. Braided black hair hung to his shoulders.

"I don't know," I said. My voice sounded funny. Slurred. He took the cup from my hand gently, sniffed it, then set it on the ground.

"Come with me," he said. I followed him. We weaved through the crowd, eventually finding the front door.

"Do you know how to get home?" He asked. I nodded. "Is it far?"

"Yeah," I said. "I live on a ranch."

"Who's ranch?"

"Paul Bauer. He's my dad."

"Hmm," the man said. He walked out into the cold. When I waited at the front door, he beckoned me.

The house or the man? Which do you choose? You've never talked with him, though you *might* have seen him in a grocery store once. You see the car he drove, an old white Lincoln two-door with rust all around it. A spider-web crack in the windshield.

You don't want to go back inside, even though the cold bites your skin. You see Emma, her half-naked body exposed through a second-story window until a pair of dark hands that don't belong to your father close the blinds. Your stomach feels sick, and for some reason, you see the snowflakes and think of Baby Jesus lying in a manger, and wish that if he were going to come back to make the whole world better like Cory said he would, that he would hurry up and do it already.

The man walks back to the door. He takes your hand gently. You feel yourself getting drowsy, so he carries you to his car. He buckles your seatbelt.

Briefly, you remember a lecture on stranger danger from a school assembly. Then you drift. Then you fall asleep.

29

I NEVER SAW THE MAN again. I woke up in my bed, wearing the same clothes as the night before. My stomach felt like I had the flu. It took me an hour to get out of bed. When I did, I walked to the front door. A brief memory came back, me stepping out of the Lincoln, and there in the snow only one set of footprints leading up to the door. They start about twenty yards from the entrance to my home as if some divine hand had set me just outside of our double-wide. No tire tracks. No enormous footprints from a buffalo man. I wonder, some nights, if he could have been an angel. I'd heard of them before, but always assumed they had wings, or at least didn't smoke the same brand of cigarettes as my father.

Whatever that man was, whatever reason I never saw the tire tracks into or out of our place, I was grateful. He had carried me home. He had given me my life. I stood for a long time that morning, just staring out at the snow. It looked so bright and pure.

***

PAUL AND EMMA hadn't come home.

Maybe they never came home. Maybe the shell that returned that evening with a raging hangover wasn't my father.

It was him, in a way. But after the party, there would never be another moment we had just us. Every time we spoke, Emma curled around our conversation, constricting, choking the words from us. No, when I saw my father that night, eyes staring into nothingness, I had seen the last images I would have of him. Even today, when I look back to those days, there is an eternal man in an eternal armchair, blinded by booze, all liquor and no life. Paul Bauer the cowboy. For those last days, he stepped into the realm of the phantoms, into the great sky of the Aurora Borealis, into that world that had passed on.

Getting to school became the main challenge in my life. For a few days, I simply missed it. Then, worrying that my not attending would cause a little too much unwanted attention from my father's least favorite sheriff, he instructed me to 'get my little butt into a desk'.

Grandma Helen, of all people, proved the most useful in this endeavor. I biked over to her restaurant, which took twenty minutes on a normal day and nearly forty in the snow. Corey was just getting into her car.

"Rosie?" he asked.

"Hey, Corey," I said. Grandma Helen walked out the front door. She glared at me. No doubt I was a reminder of the man who didn't keep her warm this winter. Her voice matched the cool air outside.

"Good morning, Samantha," she said.

"Good morning," I said formally. "Could you...would you drive me to school, please?"

"Where's your father," she demanded.

I had no answer for her. How do you tell a woman you've known your whole life that your father probably hasn't even woken up, and that when he does, he probably won't notice your absence for a few hours, if he does at all? The answer is simple: you don't. You bite your tongue and try not to cry in front of this woman you once thought to be scary, before you realized what it meant to really be scared.

Helen softened. She had been a mother once. She was still a mother, in a way, even though her daughter rested in the arms way up yonder. You can't stop being a mother any more than you can stop being a daughter. I don't say she couldn't have turned me away. She could have. But she wouldn't do that. She wouldn't leave me holding my bicycle in the cool of March.

"You can ride with me any morning, dear," she said. I leaned my bicycle against the siding and embraced her. In grief for a dying man, we were related "Go on, now. Hop in."

My morning routine became the sneaking out of the house, the ride to the restaurant, the car ride to school and safety. My stomach rumbled by ten. I forced myself to focus when I could.

Ophelia told me, in passing, that a new DSS agent would be arriving in our town a month from now.

"It should be shorter," she said. "But governments move very slowly, especially out here."

"Why are you telling me this?" I asked. I knew the answer. Because you aren't safe.

The cell phone Ophelia had given me felt heavier every day. I'm sure that she could find a way to get me off the ranch until the new agent showed up. One phone call would bring this to an end. Could foster care really be worse than living in what used to be our home? I couldn't shake the expression of that bartender in Branson a lifetime ago, but I also couldn't ignore everything that changed in my life. Papa used to sing with me, but now he had gone quiet, and the prairie seemed to be filled with only lonesome dog wails. Could I keep outrunning the coyote? Or was it the spider I ran from? Or both? Or neither?

I made that phone call one day.

Everything ended.

30

I HAD A DREAM THE night before my call. It was one of those dreams that come only once or twice in a lifetime, the type you know you'll always remember. Red skies covered the prairie. Familiar songs of creaking tin filled the air. In my dream it was harvest. Brown stalks of corn, brown soybeans, brown sunflowers draped themselves over the fields. When I looked at my arms, I didn't wear my gloves. They looked the way they did before the fire.

I stood on a gravel road between the restaurant and the ranch. A tree, still holding some of its brown, stringy leaves groaned. Faces formed and dispersed in the knotted wood. Some looked familiar. Others I couldn't place. They made no expression, only shifted in the bark and cracked wood. They were transient. Twice I counted my own face among them.

A spider, big as a horse, face unreadable, stepped from a field. It opened its mouth, and Sheriff Coulson's baritone voice came from within. I heard him with my chest. It was like his voice went through me rather than into my ears.

"You've a choice to make, girl," the Spider-Coulson said.

"Where am I?" I asked. Thunder rolled along the clouds. Red lightning followed in the distance. This out of order storm approached us. More thunder. More lightning following it.

"You've got a choice to make," the spider repeated.

"You sound funny," I said. I meant it to sound brave. It sounded hollow like a cheap movie line repeated out of context.

"You know I hunt the coyote," Coulson said.

"Why?" I demanded.

"Because I am a spider. Because he is a coyote. Must there be another reason?"

More thunder. The booms felt larger. They shook my teeth. A scream wanted to crawl out of my throat but I wouldn't let it.

"You need to ask me to get the coyote. I can carry him away to a different land where he can be free. I will do it myself if you won't help me. I will not be tricked again. I will not carry away a live coyote. I will not watch him jump from my fire."

"I love the coyote," I said. "I don't trust you. You're a liar."

"So is the coyote," the spider said, and he was right, and I could have smashed him if I could find a rock big enough.

"Choose," the spider said. It pointed a spindly leg in the direction of the restaurant. "The unknown." Then, it swung the leg towards the ranch. Cracking, the sound of bones breaking, overpowered even the boom of thunder. It sounded like gunfire. It sounded like death. "The known."

Red lightning shattered the bark of the tree. I screamed then. I made my choice.

I ran for the ranch. The lightning struck near my ankles. Charged air made my arm hair stand straight up. I knew I would die on the road. I would never reach home.

Except I did. I looked behind me and I was looking at my house. I looked down and I was in a folding steel camp chair. Another chair sat unoccupied next to me. The red sky stretched over my chunk of the prairie. The storm made little noise. It had been tamed by the sudden shift of scenery.

A coyote opened the screen door with his paw. He strutted out, all rolling shoulders and flaring nostrils. The Spider-Coulson had surprised and frightened me. This creature did not. I knew its steps, knew the gentle slope of its shoulders, knew that this trickster, who got so far with lying and deception, only ever hurt itself in the end, that it could not forever outrun the spider. When this animal jumped into the chair, I knew whose voice would come from that mouth.

"Hey, Lemondrop," my coyote-father said. His voice came out clear and kind, with no slur that seemed so commonplace now.

"Hey, Papa," I said. I felt a lump form in my throat and tried to swallow it.

"You look scared, girl," he said.

"I am," I replied. It was true. Three sounds filled the distance: grass fire's soft crackle, the rush of chlorinated water in a too-deep pool, and the tick of a propane heater not lighting. "I'm very scared."

"I am too," my father said. A whimper escaped his animal lips. "I'm very scared too."

"You aren't afraid of anything," I said.

"Yes I am," he said. He cried out. "I'm scared of my own shadow. I'm a scaredy-coyote." He hopped off the chair and covered his face with his paws. I laughed. He popped out and grinned. "There's my girl."

"I met the sheriff," I said. His face grew long. He looked sad.

"The spider, huh?"

"Yeah."

"Gave you a choice?"

"He did." I looked up at the sky. "I came back here."

"I wish you hadn't," he said quietly. I felt tears in my eyes, and I saw them in his.

"I don't trust him," I said.

"I wish so much for you, Lemondrop." The storm approached again. What I had thought had been a taming was only a temporary respite.

"I heard another story," Papa said. His coyote eyes looked to the red clouds above the land. "Not from an Indian. I heard it from my mother, but it wasn't something she was told. She learned it herself."

"Did she drink," I asked.

"All the time." He shook his head. "She should have been a fish. She should have lived in the ocean where there is only water. This American desert doesn't have enough water, so she drank whiskey."

It made my heart sad to hear about my grandmother.

"I asked her why she chose to live here." Papa pointed his paw out at our ranch. The ramshackle buildings looked haunted in the red evening. Piles of steel became ghouls. Loaders covered in tall grass became vicious animals. As he spoke, rattling filled the air. A cacophony of danger completed itself with that rhythm hiss.

Thunder. Ticking. Creaking. Burning. Rattling.

"My mama, she said she didn't look at things much. Wore thick glasses. We called 'em coke bottles. But she listened. Her world was a soundscape. Then she held my hand, I weren't no bigger than you, and she said, 'I liked the prairie song. It sounds like the voice of your father'. It was the only time she ever mentioned him." The source of the rattle slithered up our porch. I pulled my legs up into my chair. On the back of the snake, goading it on, rode Iktomi, which was Coulson, which was the eight-legged death. My father turned his sad coyote eyes to me. "I liked our songs together."

He jumped from the chair and growled at the snake. It lunged, sinking fangs into his neck. His jaws found the middle of the cursed creature. They clamped down hard. The snake writhed in his mouth, but he refused to let go, even though it was killing him.

The snake split in two. The dead rattle fell to the ground first. Papa shook his mane until the head dropped to the dirt. Blood dripped from the hair on his mouth.

"I'm sorry, coyote," Coulson said. I tried to step on him, but he was too quick. His little legs carried him back onto the prairie, leaving me alone with the dying coyote.

The song continued in the night air, but incomplete and ugly. Papa stood and took a few shaky steps before falling to the ground. I rushed to him then. I held his face in my hands, ignorant of the blood that was now falling on my palms.

"It doesn't sound right," I said. "The songs don't sound right without you."

"Only one more song," Papa said, his voice strained. "Everything ends, girl. Even the music. Enjoy it while it lasts."

He raised his head with considerable effort. Then he added his coyote cry to the prairie, and he left me.

31

I WOKE IN A COLD sweat. My father snored in the other room. I put on my gloves as I did every morning. It felt so odd, to wake from a nightmare into a nightmare, and wonder at how the one you knew to be fake could feel more real. I sat on my bed for a long time, pondering what such a dream could mean. I never remembered my dreams, but this one stuck in my mind like a post in the dirt. It still does to this day.

I looked at the phone on my stand. I could call Ophelia now. But I didn't. Actions not taken. I thought being awake was enough for life, that I could just be ready for the spider this time.

Snow still hung in piles in ditches here or there, but mostly it had left us behind. Spring wandered back into our lives. Another Dakota tradition: on the first really nice day after a particularly brutal winter, everyone wanted to be outside. We went to school and passed the time staring out the windows and ignoring a well-meaning teacher. When class finally got out, we sprinted for Grandma Helen's roaring car. I sat in the back seat next to Corey. Puffy white clouds dotted our blue sky. Life might have been a good dream.

"Let's go hunt snakes," Corey said. It sounded like the best idea in the whole world.

We jumped from the car the moment it came to a complete stop. Grandma Helen laughed at our giddiness as we ran for our bikes.

"Just be safe now. You be back before dark, Corey." She strolled inside. We didn't wait for her. The wind took my hair as we approached the highway. For the first day in months, the only thought on my mind wasn't what I rode home to. Instead, it was on exploring all our old favorite pastures.

Our wheels kicked up a trail of dust. Corey let out an ear-splitting whoop, and I did the same. We were a lord and lady of the prairie. We owned the rolling grasslands. We ruled the dirt fields and the waving trees. Enthroned on mechanical horses, we became the riders we saw on television screens. Corey and I rode our bikes to the ranch. We rode towards death.

The cows greeted us as we rolled in. They looked thinner than they had before Emma. Papa didn't abandon his chores every day, but he had done so enough times that the ribs of the cattle were visible now. They made me melancholy. I didn't let my eyes linger on them.

Perhaps that was a sin I committed. I looked away from something in pain.

EmEm's car was parked next to my father's, the same place I had left it this morning. They had gotten into a spat over money before I left. I caught a few words through their door. I ignored it as best I could.

Something shifted in my heart. Seeing her car parked in the same place she always parked and realizing that was 'her spot' made my blood boil. I looked at Corey.

"You want to hunt snakes?" I asked.

"Yeah," he said slowly. He knew me long enough to recognize an off tone of my voice.

"Wait here," I ordered. We left our bikes next to the porch. I went inside.

My father and Emma lay together on the couch, snoring. The TV played 'Ghostbusters II'. His arm was draped over her shoulder. They looked the part of the happy couple. I could almost ignore that neither of them wore shirts, that my father's teeth sat on the coffee table, that he had twenty years of age on her if one rounded down by a lot. Thankfully, their regular party attendees were nowhere to be seen. I crept into my father's room.

He didn't even keep it locked up. His queen bed had a cabinet on either side of the headboard. Inside the one nearest the door, glinting in the sunlight that peered through his plastic curtains, was a silver Colt .45. It was a big iron on my father's hip, the cowboy gun complete with snakeskin grips. I had shot it once. The recoil frightened me then. It didn't now. When my fingers wrapped around the handle, I noticed the contrast between the black fabric that hid my scars and the tan diamondback pattern. I opened the cylinder the way Papa had taught me. He kept it loaded at all times. I grabbed a box of shells just in case we wanted more than six shots.

I tiptoed out into the living room. Emma stirred but didn't wake. I slid through the screen door.

Corey stared at the silver pistol.

"What?" I asked.

"You shouldn't have that," he said. I glared at him.

"Why not?"

"You shouldn't have it," he said. "We shouldn't mess with that."

I strutted down the steps. My finger jabbed into his chest. He recoiled.

"Don't be a pussy," I said. I liked the feeling of being mean. I liked the feeling of being in charge. His eyes moved from me to the pistol to the front door. He hoped my father would walk out, scold us both for holding his prized possession, maybe even ground us. He wanted a grown-up to do something.

There were no grown-ups around.

"I'm going snake hunting. We do it all the time, and we never get anything. Well, I want a rattle, so I'm bringing a gun. That's that. You can come with, or bike on home."

Corey looked once more to the door that would never produce a savior and nodded.

"I'll go with you."

We trudged through the mud. The snow might be melting, but it didn't leave the ground. It stayed beneath the dirt, making it cling to our shoes. We moved towards a tree line, our ears tuning in to the sounds of nature around us. We wanted to hear the shake of snaketail. All we got was the squish of mud. We made it to the edge of the property. A line of barbed wire delineated where our pasture ended and the neighbors began. From here, Gabriel's house was closer than mine. I looked down at the place where I fell. The barn no longer stood. My hands, my arms, the ugly scars, they hadn't saved anything. They happened. No reason remained. Only the fact of the ache, the damage. I looked at my gloved hands.

I pulled the left one off first, then the right. I threw them on the ground and stomped them into the mud.

"Are you alright?" Corey asked. I shook my head. Then, angrily, I showed him the backs of my hands.

"Do I look alright?"

"Don't wave the gun like that," he said. "I don't care!" I shouted. He grabbed my hands.

"I care. And I don't care about your hands." We both looked down. He held both of mine in both of his. I blushed with shame. We never yelled at each other. That's not what friends did.

"Thanks," I said. He released my hands. I wiped my nose.

We heard it then.

A rattle.

Ten feet from us, tan against black earth, a coil of mama rattlesnake baring its fangs. I pressed the pistol into Corey's hand.

"You get it."

"Me?" he asked, trying to refuse the gun. I wrapped his fingers around the handle.

"You get it." I nodded at him. "It was your idea to hunt snakes the first time anyway."

He took the pistol. I showed him where the sights were and how to look down and line them up.

I never once blamed him for everything that came after.

His tiny arm shook a little with the weight of the gun. The front of the barrel dipped down. Corey steadied the gun with a second hand. The snake's rattle continued.

"Shoot him, Corey," I said. He squeezed the trigger.

The noise rang in our ears. Corey barely managed to hold on to the pistol, but he did hold on, a testament to the young boy's strength. Dirt flew in the air. The snake flew up with it, a strip of skin along the middle holding two halves together. It writhed on the ground. We'd actually gotten a snake.

I jumped up and down, shaking him by the shoulder. He jumped too. We had slayed the great danger of the prairie. The rulers of the land had finally earned their title. The world could only...

Another bang. More ringing. Corey had never even held a gun before today. He had no training. He had no idea he was supposed to keep his finger away from the trigger when he wasn't aiming at something. As excitement filled the air, he accidentally squeezed his whole fist tighter, including the index finger that rested on the trigger of a double-action revolver.

Pain flared up in my foot. Blood seeped into the mud. The pain grew in intensity. Corey threw the pistol away from him.

"I'm sorry," he said. "I didn't mean to! I'm sorry!"

"Grab the gun," I said. "My dad'll kill me if he sees I took it."

"You're bleeding," he said in a panic. I was caught in a strange situation. I was the one with a hole in my fucking foot, and I had to calm him down.

"Corey. Get. The. Pistol. Now." I sat down in the mud. I didn't care if my pants got dirty at that point. He retrieved it. Using his T-shirt, he cleaned the muck from the divots in the steel. I pulled a cell phone from my pocket. Ophelia picked up after the first ring.

"Sam?"

"Opie," I couldn't keep the pain from my voice. "Come get me. I got hurt. Come pick me up. I think I need to go to the doctor."

"I'm sending Ralph," she said. It had never occurred to me that our sheriff had a first name. I laughed. The whole thing was too absurd not to. My addict father left a gun unsecured in his bedroom. He slept on the couch with the world's best enabler. My best friend had just shot me. My librarian told me the sheriff's name was Ralph. It seemed like the funniest thing in the world. "Is this a prank, Sam?"

Corey took the phone. "It's not. She's shot. I...I shot her on accident."

"Where?" Ophelia said so loud I heard her. The worry in her voice brought me out of my laughing fit. The pain seemed so much more pronounced now. I groaned.

"In the foot. We're at her ranch. Out in the pasture."

"Corey Hoffman, you listen careful. You get her to the house. When you get there, you wrap her foot in a towel and you put pressure on it. Say you understand."

"I understand," Corey said.

"I have to go. I have to call Ralph. Get her to the house."

Corey put the phone in his pocket. He helped me up. I had to put my arm around him. He walked to my injured side. I used his body as a crutch, hopping one foot forward. It took us forever, which was probably only ten minutes, but we made it to the base of our driveway. My father, a shirt hanging open, hat haphazard on his head, saw Corey and me. He ran for us.

"What happened?" He shouted.

"We were hunting snakes..." I began. Papa saw the pistol in Corey's hand. He snatched it from Corey.

"Did you do this to my daughter?" He checked the pistol. I remember seeing him sway on his feet, not close to sober, loaded as a gun. Corey, the idiot, chose that moment to tell the truth.

"We were out hunting snakes. I accidentally pulled the trigger."

My father grabbed his shirt and pulled him forward. I fell to the ground. Pain shot through my leg. I screamed.

"You shot my girl?" Corey had to stand on his tiptoes. My papa was lifting him off the ground. The dirt beneath me felt alien. Was this the land I grew up in? Something had turned sour here. Something had abandoned us to our fate. I heard the slur in his voice. Almost all of the ingredients for our disaster were present. Booze or worse, an injury, a pistol. All we needed was the car that pulled into the driveway.

Papa barely registered the flashing lights. He didn't register the sound of a vehicle slamming on the brakes, the door swinging wide, the immense man stepping into the dust, his car wailing like a horse that smells trouble. No, Paul's attention was fixed on my best friend.

"You shot my little girl?" The fact that his little girl lay in the mud a mere two feet from him, writhing in pain, didn't seem to register. He wasn't my father. He was all rage, all booze, all hate. He jabbed the barrel of the gun in Corey's ribs.

"Paul!" Sheriff Coulson boomed. His door was open. The lights flashed to his right, casting his features in an alternating red or blue war paint. He had his weapon drawn. "Drop the gun, Paul. You don't want to hurt that boy, now."

The third standoff at the Bauer Ranch, only this time it wasn't words in holsters but iron. It could have been the climax, a camera zoom towards the eyes, one set steeled, the other glassed over. Music might have swelled as the scene cut between the two men of the prairie. Corey struggled. My father was hurting him. All I could think about was pain. I wanted to go home. I was home, but I wasn't. This didn't seem right. I hurt. I felt like my mind had been sent back in time to the day of the fire. Only details made it through. It was as if someone took the complete jigsaw puzzle of reality and tossed it in the air. The trees. Coulson's brown boots. Sweat on my father's forehead. Corey's hair blowing in the wind.

"Put him down, Paul," Coulson ordered. "Nothing bad has happened yet."

Everything bad had happened. You're old enough to know how these movies go. Guns were already drawn. When a pistol makes it out of a holster, you know that John Wayne is either going to kill or be killed. He doesn't draw a gun for show.

Coulson and my father, both men in the place men like them belonged, both stuck in a time that didn't have space for cowboys. This was the West dying. This was the last Dakota war. This was our final twitching fingers before the death.

Papa looked at me on the ground, holding my foot. He made a face, and I knew that he was dead when he did.

"No!" I shouted.

"Get off my land!" Papa shouted.

Sheriff Coulson didn't speak.

When the barrel of Paul's pistol moved towards the police car, the sheriff's gun thundered over the prairie. Corey dropped to the ground. Coulson moved forward. He looked at my father, crumpled on the ground like a rabid coyote that had to be put down, and grimaced.

"Is anyone in the house," he said. I was numb. I stared at my father. Sheriff Coulson picked Corey up off the ground. "Get her to the car." He moved towards the house, gun lower but still drawn.

Corey didn't help me up. He stood still. Then, as Coulson entered the house, my friend dropped to the ground next to me. He reached his hand out. It found mine.

There it is. My hand in his hand. The soft palm. The nervous tremor. Each of us unsure of how anything could ever go right again. His hand. My hand. Holding on to the world is impossible when you're that age. But holding each other, even for a moment, that was something. I stared at my father. He seemed to me the last real cowboy then, from his hat down to his boots.

How Whiskey Made the Coyote Sing

Part IV

"I'd stay in the garden with Him
Tho' the night around me be falling;
But He bids me go; thro' the voice of woe,
His voice to me is calling.

-C. Austin Miles, performed by Elvis Presley, Johnny Cash, Alan Jackson, Randy Travis, and many others.

32

THE REST OF THE DAY is a blur. Coulson shouted at Corey for not getting me into the car, but I don't remember that, nor do I remember riding next to a handcuffed EmEm all the way to the hospital. After the flash of Coulson's gun, I time-travel to a day later, my foot wrapped in white, a doctor looking down on me.

They brought me food, which I rarely ate. When I slept, I woke up screaming, unable to remember whatever nightmare tormented me. I wept randomly, without cause, unsure of any reason, until all the tears in the universe were cried out of me.

The new agent, two days too late, too late to save my father, sat in one of the hospital chairs. She asked me questions which I refused to answer. She smoked inside until a doctor hollered at her. She had mean eyes.

It was she, not Ophelia, who drove me back to the ranch. As we walked in, her nasally voice said only one thing.

"Pack what you need. We won't come back here again."

Back here. Back to the place where we listened to Bob Dylan or Waylon Jennings or Willie Nelson. Back to the living room where Totino's Pizza felt like fine dining. Back to the place where my father stood tall, outlined in halogen lights, a real man of the prairie, smelling like aftershave, like alcohol, where I once laughed as The Apple Dumpling Gang played on our old television, where we were family, that is where I could never go back. But I wanted to go back. I had wanted it for years.

I made my way through the garbage strewn corpse of our home. I packed few things, some clothes, my toothbrush, a spare pair of shoes.

There, hanging on a hook, was the purse my father had bought me in Branson. I had more than enough room. I could leave it there, and abandon even the good. Or I could take it with me.

I can't tell you which I did. I am ashamed.

Sheriff Coulson stayed away from the funeral. Ophelia sat with me, and I held her hand so tightly my fingernails left marks on her skin.

They dressed him in a suit. I hated that suit, and the looks the regular attendees of the Presbyterian church gave me, and the music they played. When they sounded Amazing Grace, it didn't sound like his voice, hoarse, echoing in the cab of our Chevy pickup. It didn't sound like Tuesday mornings with sprinkles in my pancakes or evenings dancing in the living room of a double-wide that might not win any beauty contests but *dammit it was ours*. That's what a funeral should be: all the good and none of the bad, or if you have to have the bad, a reminder that there was so much love. There was once a time when my father loved me, and none of them could see it. Even Opie could only sit like a tree in the midst of an ocean of grass, as solid as she was unable to understand.

I wish I could tell you that afterward, I moved in with her, that we became a real family, that Corey and I grew up together every day, and all was right in the world.

It wouldn't be the truth. The truth is that I had to say goodbye to Corey outside of the service station, a government-owned Crown Victoria idling behind me. Tears stained his dirty face, and that boy was so beautiful when he grieved what we lost because he was like me. Of all the people in the world, he understood that the Child Services agent smoking camel crushes would take me to a new land, where cowboys didn't order hamburgers from one-handed grandmothers. This was our end. I hugged him so hard. I prayed a simple prayer in his ear.

"If, one day, you can ride your bike to where I'm at, we'll still be friends. We'll always still be friends."

They pushed me into the foster system, and the rest of what childhood I had was spent with little stability or companionship. They rotated me through homes across the state. There were Christians sometimes, people who took me to church, but mostly there were people who cared as little for my soul as my personhood. No place ever got as bad as Emma on the couch, lines of not-sugar, different party-goers all looking for the same substitute for reality.

Some days I thought of Corey, and Lemmon, and Ophelia, and Coulson, and my father. The pain festered like a sore. I felt as if I were a mare with a broke leg. I couldn't seem to keep moving down the trail in the same way. So I did my best to hobble.

Sometimes kids laughed at my gloves, or my limp, or my old lady cane. Others had eyes filled with so much pity that my blood boiled whenever they turned them to me. Introversion came naturally, a byproduct of the nights in different beds, of the longing for a friend who still lived where I came from but never seemed to get back to.

It's as much a part of my song as the rest, the different houses, the rotating faces, and not a single one a man like my father. That day on the ranch, his cockeyed hat lying in the prairie dust, the west died with him. The world died with him.

Yet I had food. You may know the feeling, you may not. I had regular meals. I had a warm place to sleep at night. Never again did I have to start a propane heater in a prairie winter. Never again did I have to drive a water truck towards the gaping maw of a prairie fire. This new world of webbing, this world where the spider-state told me where to live, it held me down, but it held me down with a roof over my head, with no drinking except for a beer with a football game, no homes where men's hands drug across me, no women telling me to keep secrets from cops, no driving drunk adults home on my birthday. This new world taught me to hobble. It taught me to keep moving. Above all, it taught me about what it could be like to live in a place where love might be gone but at least security stayed.

My eighteenth birthday came with the understanding that I was to find my own place in their world. I didn't struggle to transition to adulthood, not really. When you've done what I've done from such a young age, apartment rent doesn't scare you.

School still fascinated me, even though I didn't graduate from a traditional route. My birthday is around Christmas, and for my present the year I turned eighteen, I bought a one-way ticket to New York, nothing but a notebook and a dream.

New York meant a chance to make the world something living, far from the long sightlines of the Midwest. It meant leaving my silent prairie behind. No song ever sounded the same there. I made the world alive by looking away, by clogging my ears with taxi horns or hobos preaching the coming messiah. I moved to a city where buildings blocked the view of the great beyond that made you feel small. A skyscraper might be enormous, but it pales in comparison to the big skies over the plains. I needed a place where everything could be held in my own two hands again.

My first job didn't care that I didn't have a diploma. Dishwashers didn't need degrees, according to the little Italian hiring manager. The first day there, I tied my apron, secured my hair net, and removed my gloves. I heard the voice of one of the cooks over the din of the dinner rush.

"Holy shit."

33

I RECOGNIZED THE SWAGGER MORE than the man. His face didn't age kindly. Long worry canyons snaked along his cheeks. Skin hung haggard around him. Yet the man still carried himself like the room would listen when his mouth spat numbers quick as a repeating rifle. Some quiet Saturday, carried in by the sound of traffic and a gust of November cold, Lionel Richards, the man my father used to tease because of a shared name with an elevator musician, strolled into my New York Diner.

The little Italian man, Enzo, raised his bushy eyebrows when I said I intended to take a lunch break. I had worked there for months, and not once had I taken so much as five minutes for a cigarette with the cooks. Say what you will about the Midwestern attitude: we know how to work.

Lionel started when I sat down. Up close, he looked even older. He had lost his Pringle's can mustache along with a hundred pounds. A green-topped oxygen tank trailed him like a faithful hound. The bolo tie around his neck looked tarnished. Lionel lived within the word haggard. Even so, yellow teeth broke into a smile.

"I thought that I would run into you again."

"You recognize me?" I asked, not bothering to hide my surprise.

"How could I forget you, Sammy?" He was in town to see his brother and go over papers, the kind that people needed after. I waved to the waiter and ordered us some omelets. He took his with 'all the fixins'. I asked for a side of pancakes with sprinkles. It felt sentimental, us sitting in the diner, even though neither of us had ever seen the other outside of the sales. This chance at conversation meant a chance to look back to the little girl from Lemmon, all the oily machinery, even that day he stood before my father with a lean to his body and no salvation in his words. Coward Lionel, victim Sammy, breakfast. It all felt terribly important. Sometimes the ordinary gets that way. I like to think that we glimpse the meaning of it all in those moments: we both knew that this would be the last chance to speak about what had happened. We both knew that this was the goodbye we never got.

"Lungs," he said before taking a mouthful of hash browns. "Both of them. Eight months of chemo and we're worse than when we started."

"I'm sorry," I said, and I meant it.

"You have to admit there's a kind of irony there. I got my money's worth out of the old airbags. God must've thought I'd used them enough."

"Hmm," I said, unsure of what to say. What can you say? He must have seen it in my face.

"This ain't something to feel sorry for. This is life. Find a point if you can, or don't, it ends just the same." He had become bitter by then, fed up with the hand he had been dealt, unable to bluff and knowing it. We were adults, so I asked about work.

"I suppose you're out of the sales business then," I said. Lionel shook his head at the question. From sunken sockets, his eyes peered out at me, measuring my mood. We both knew what he needed. How to say it, though? How to drag it out? A pleasant meal, a few anecdotes about prairie winters, this could be everything between us. He could stand up, grab his pathetic little steel tank, and drag himself from my diner and my life. It would be the cowardly thing to do. If I'm honest, it's what I expected of him.

Yet my old friend had one last surprise for me.

"I had a sister. Sarah. She was an addict," he said softly. "Two years after Paul...two years after your father passed, we found her in her apartment. She OD'd." He pulled a cross from his neck, and slid it across the table to me. "This was hers."

I examined the necklace. It was a solid gold piece, chain and all, with diamonds on the crucifix.

"I thought God was punishing me," he said.

"For what?"

"For that day. For not saying something." Lionel wouldn't meet my eye. "Only ever thought the same thing one other time, the day I got diagnosed. I thought God hadn't forgotten what I'd done. No siree. He keeps it all in his little book. And when the bill comes due, sometimes you owe a hell of a lot."

The diner continued. The traffic continued. The world outside continued. It doesn't know how to do anything else. Slowly, I removed my gloves. Lionel covered his mouth.

"Oh God," he said. "Oh God, Sam, I wish so much that I had just called somebody."

So he said it. So he knew. So everyone must have known all along. This is the truth, that when a person is blind to some things, it's because they chose to be.

"But you didn't," I said. Some part of the song still lived in my lungs, probably still lived in the pair that rotted in his chest. The song sang the truth. Life isn't how we wish it. Life is how we live it.

I took one of his hands in mine. He nearly choked trying to say the next words.

"Do you hate him?"

That was the question. My fingers all scar tissue, my hands deformed, these things that help me reach out permanently changed by the years beneath the Dakota sky, God the holy father answering so few of my prayers, all of this asking me one question.

"It was nice to see you," I said.

“I won’t do it again,” he said. Lionel clenched his teeth. He held my hand in his. He looked directly in my eyes. “I’m sorry, Sam. I’m sorry for everything.”

Then he cried. I wonder still if God heard him.

***

I COULDN’T WORK at the diner after that day. More jobs came and went. I took on a secretary job at a small paper manufacturer. The work came in waves, and during the slow times, I would write.

My first book was an entry novel to a series about a snake hunter turned archaeologist. She realized she never liked hunting live things anyway. It landed me my first agent, who I still have to this day. He said it had ‘real fire’ to it. All I cared about was the ‘real paycheck’ that got me out of scheduling meetings or emails about shipments to Biwabik, Minnesota.

Some nights I was lonely. I would go to sit in bars, listening to the movement of an eight million person city, and wonder how long the party could go on without looking the bottles in the eye. How many of the men and women grinding to a Bruno Mars song were once children who watched Spongebob with their fathers, who wondered where their mothers went sometimes, who missed the way the song used to sing across their homelands in the beauty of the evening sky?

You know the ending, I think, or at least hoped for it. I know I did on those crowded nights, people like locusts across the face of the earth. I prayed for it on a bar stool. Call it coincidence. Call it God. All I know was that it had been decades since I had wanted anything so badly.

He visited me one day. We reconnected over Facebook, that beautiful, terrible invention. At first, I thought it wasn’t possible. So much of that life had passed on. But Corey Bruce Hoffman, he was still somehow a reality, even after all the life that happened between our rushed goodbye and the hectic now.

The summer before I turned twenty, he rode his Harley Davidson to the Big Apple. I thought he looked every bit the hick I had been two years prior.

This part is predictable. The first meeting felt easy. But when I hugged him, he cried. He apologized a lot. I told him to get over it, but we both knew I didn't mean it. You don't get over something like that. You don't move on from the lives we lived.

He confided in me about the loneliness after I left, how he never did fit in with the rest of the kids there, how his grandmother never did move past the death of her own daughter or stop blaming him for it. As easily as riding a bike, we slipped back into the jokes of childhood. We were again friends with a disparity, one knowing a small slice of reality, the other all too happy to share what was really out there. Only this time, I could be the one to teach him about the great wide world.

I took him to the library first. He couldn't believe it.

We wandered the halls. It felt so good to be together. I didn't have to explain my limp or my gloves. Why would I? He was there for it. Continuity is so often overlooked, but its power is real. It's felt in the ease of gentle conversation, of the absence of discomforting questions.

He was supposed to spend a week. Then it became two. Then three. Somehow, neither of us could come up with a reason to split apart once we had found one another. Our life, our little life, became something neither of us thought possible. We found each other. We found a way to be whole again, to hold hands with someone who knew the shape of your palm, who wished the world for you. When I told him I wanted to go to college even though I already had two books published, he didn't ask me why. He knew how much school meant to me.

I married him. He asked me on a trip to the Statue of Liberty. We said our vows at a courthouse, with a few classmates from my creative writing classes as witnesses.

Life became natural. It became mundane. We bickered over trivialities. I worried about the rising price of groceries. I sold many more books in a very successful set of children's novels. He got a job in construction so he could be outside, where he always felt the world made sense. We listened to music, usually Rock and Roll, on old vinyl records. We tried to forget about it all, which both of us knew was an impossibility.

One day I vomited at three in the morning. The test showed the right number of lines. He set me on the breakfast bar and kissed me fiercely. I decided on names if it were a boy or a girl while he made us cups of tea. If we had a son, Corey Junior would be just fine by me.

A nagging had taken hold of my thoughts, though. The idea that you can't shake the past, not really. The knowledge of where you come from always affects where you're going.

I came from my father.

When I discussed these feelings with my therapist, he suggested a different kind of project. He told me to drag my father into the light. So that's what I did. Now, a year after our little Ophelia opened her own little eyes in this world, I near the end.

I've tried to come up with some 'Aha' moment for this book. I'm sure Rupie would love some grand moral, my villainous father crucified before the nations. All that would be required would be my words. I can hear my publicist's voice, so like the voice of a sheriff-spider, whispering in my ear.

Just say it. Just say that you hate him.

But I don't. I didn't, and I don't. That's the nature of the whole damned thing. I relived the bars, the mornings, the heartache of seeing that he couldn't follow the words coming out of my mouth because they were filtered through a fifth of Jack Daniels. I saw the endless rotation of men in our home, the way they undressed me with their eyes, the things Emma did. I went back through the lands I once lived, and I don't hate him.

I can feel how you feel, even through these pages. I can feel your condemnation. Why not? The man was a monster. He brought hell into our home. He left me places. He forgot me in places. He drank paychecks away. He pouted like a toddler. You judge him for that.

Fine.

But you didn't do anything about it either.

You just sat back and watched.

My father drank whiskey in the truck, and I loved him anyway. I wept at his funeral. Would you not mourn him because of his flaws? It's the only way I can mourn him. It's the only way he was.

Acknowledgments

This book would not have been possible without the support of my many friends and family members. Though these few acknowledgments may exclude some, know that while the act of writing is a solitary process, the act of life is a communal experience. I am beyond blessed to have such a wonderful community surrounding me.

Special thanks must be given to Molly Erickson, Lanelle McCallister, Brett Erickson, and Sarah Krempges for their time and effort reading this novel before it had been polished. Like the world of farming in the Midwest, this book no doubt has many rough edges or rust spots. Their contributions played an enormous role in limiting the amount of imperfections from making it to print.

My cover artist, Emma Hiyashi, has done tremendous work on this project.

I also want to extend my sincerest thanks to my friends Dante VanBeek, Dan and Emily Moe, Jaedon and Sam Hoff, Micah and Brenna Rens, Isaac and Abby Anderson, Braden Tieszen, Ben and Mikayla Dykstra, Jacob Wingert, Bailey and Lauren VandeGriend, Conner and Camryn Watley, Creighton Watley, and Ian and Cade Engbrecht for their continuing support of my writing career. Their patience and kindness knows no bounds.

For my brothers, their wives, and their lovely children, as well as my loving parents, I am immeasurably grateful.

There is love for you. There will always be love.

Want to read more of Joshua Erickson's work? He can be found at:

- Instagram: @authorjoshuaerickson

- TikTok: @authorjoshuaerickson

- Web: www.authorjoshuaerickson.com

-YouTube: @authorjoshuaerickson

He would also appreciate if you review this book on amazon or goodreads!

www.ingramcontent.com/pod-product-compliance
Lightning Source LLC
Chambersburg PA
CBHW030809310726
48980CB00006B/432/J

* 9 7 9 8 9 9 2 3 7 7 1 0 1 *